"Until we have absolute proof one way or the other, the Mothman will remain like Bigfoot, Nessie and other 'monsters' ... elusive."
– Carrie McCabe, co-host of the "Ain't it Scary? with Sean & Carrie" podcast

SYSTEMA PARADOXA

ACCOUNTS OF CRYPTOZOOLOGICAL IMPORT

VOLUME 28

MOUNT MISERY

A TALE OF THE MOTHMAN

AS ACCOUNTED BY JAMES CHAMBERS

ILLUSTRATED BY JW HARP

NEOPARADOXA

Pennsville, NJ

2025

PUBLISHED BY
NeoParadoxa
A division of eSpec Books
PO Box 242
Pennsville, NJ 08070
www.especbooks.com

Copyright © 2025 James Chambers

ISBN: 978-1-965266-25-0
ISBN (ebook): 978-1-965266-24-3

All rights reserved. No part of the contents of this book may be reproduced or transmitted in any form or by any means without the written permission of the publisher.

All persons, places, and events in this book are fictitious and any resemblance to actual persons, places, or events is purely coincidental.

Interior Design: Danielle McPhail
www.sidhenadaire.com

Cover Art: JW Harp
Cover Design: Mike and Danielle McPhail, McP Digital Graphics
Interior Illustration: JW Harp

Copyediting: Greg Schauer and John L. French

Dedication

For Melanie

FOREWORD

Life often echoes itself—and last December mine reverberated with thunderous ripples of chaotic, hidden forces that had twice before blasted through into my orderly world.

It began, literally, with a ringing.

One cold evening as the Earth crept toward the darkest day of the year, the landline I hardly used anymore jangled for attention. I answered it to staticky silence.

After several greetings failed to bring a response, I hung up.

The phone rang again before I even lifted my fingertips from the plastic. Again, silence.

I dropped it in its cradle only for the cycle to repeat. After offering several hellos, asking who was there, and hearing no reply, I decided to unplug the damn thing—but then, with the halting tone of a non-English speaker pronouncing words phonetically, a faint voice responded: "A call will come. It must be answered. Those who hear must listen."

I asked the speaker their name, who would call and when, but the voice only repeated the exact words once before disconnecting.

I set the phone in its cradle and awaited more ringing. None came.

The next morning, a gloomy, overcast, wet sort of December day, when gray mist hangs all about, but the sky never brings itself to bleed rain, I noticed an unwanted companion on my drive to the post office to mail holiday packages. A black car, with tinted windows all around and outdated black-and-gold New York license plates, followed me. I didn't recognize the make or model. It resembled a classic luxury sedan from the '60s or '70s, but with all its edges rounded and its burliness condensed to mimic contemporary, generic, rubber-stamped car bodies.

I had seen such vehicles before; so had old friends of mine, Benjamin Keep, and his wife, Annetta Maikels. They represented things I didn't wish returned to my life. I assumed they felt the same. Hoping the car might be some new hybrid from an upstart manufacturer, I added a few random turns to my route, watching for my follower to diverge — but it didn't. No matter how fast or slow I drove, no matter how often I nudged the gas or tapped the brake, it tailed me at a perfectly consistent distance. Its darkened windshield concealed the driver, but I could guess what he looked like: a pale man with nondescript, almost protean features, wearing a black suit and hat.

At the post office, the car parked across the street while I completed my errand. Then it trailed me home. As I approached my driveway, I floored the gas, cut the wheel, and screeched to a stop in front of my garage, then jumped out to see the vehicle as it passed my house.

Empty road stretched in both directions. The car, four houses behind me when I'd parked, too far to pass from sight in the few seconds it took me to vacate my driver's seat, had simply vanished. Dread washed over me, a slow, rolling wave filling me up with cold. I shivered on my way to my front door — and there I halted as fresh ripples of unease crashed through me.

A shoebox sat on the front porch.

Beat-up, unwrapped, and bearing no markings other than the logo of a sneaker brand and faded size labels, it deepened my sense of peril. I gazed at it, wrestling with what to do. I could ignore the package, enter my home through another door, pretend it did not exist, and hope when I checked later, it would be gone. I could dump it into the garbage pail, unopened. I could burn it, bury it, or drive it to the nearby beach and toss it into the outgoing tide.

Or I could bring it inside and open it.

The last option made my skin crawl, but from the other time such a mysterious package appeared on my front porch, I knew the best way to resolve life's mysteries is often by working through them, not running from them — even if we never fully understand the resolution. Whoever delivered the odd package would hardly be deterred by my indifference. The more I resisted, the more they would make their presence felt. They had already signaled their desires by phone, then by black car, and now this — a series of escalations that would only continue if I ignored them.

My decision made, I deposited the damp box on my desk then stepped away to hang up my coat and mentally prepare for what it might contain.

Having walked the edges of the strange, the inexplicable, and the horrifying in the course of writing Devil in the Green and The Billabong Trail, I had no wish to return to the path. Fate, however, relishes disregarding our desires. With these few odd things having surfaced in my life, I anticipated that Ben Keep and Annetta Maikels would soon follow. Faithful readers know how

I documented Ben and Annetta's encounters with the Montauk Monster, Bigfoot, and the Men in Black, who monitor the intersections of realities, then went on to write about their investigation into the Australian cryptid, the Bunyip, and the Men Who Are Not There. In each case, I strove to recreate Ben's voice based on documents, photos, recordings, video, and other material he provided for my research.

While Devil in the Green *elicited a storm of heated response from believers, critics, seekers, and skeptics,* The Billabong Trail *seemed only to inspire anxiety. The few messages I received after publication expressed concern for my well-being and that of Ben and Annetta. Others fretted over the nature of our haunted universe and humanity's place in it, worried about what catastrophe we might instigate by probing into secrets better left undisturbed. Perhaps the carnivorous Bunyip, the irrational acts of the Men Who Aren't There, and the sub-dimensional reach of the Billabong Trail — which seemed to connect literal opposite ends of the earth — gave too stark a glimpse into what lies beneath the veneer of reality.*

All this left me deeply reluctant to write another account of Ben and Annetta's ventures. But I saw no other course to follow. What happened when I opened the box, when I reconnected with Ben and Annetta several weeks later, and heard their story, I've recorded as faithfully as possible in the following pages. Once more, I've attempted to capture Ben's experience and voice, to tell his and Annetta's story, not my own. As in the past, Ben agreed to share salient bits of hard evidence with my publisher to ensure her that this story captures events worthy of public knowledge. This time, my editor barely listened to the recordings, hardly skimmed the documents, discouraged from delving too much into the material by incidents of weirdness that have crept into her life after reviewing Ben's and Annetta's materials for our last two projects.

Readers, make of this story what you will. Some of you will believe. Some will scoff. Some will dismiss. So that skeptics don't feel cheated, I've endeavored, above all, to make this entertaining. Even the most ardent doubters grasp that fiction contains kernels of truth whether on the surface or sub rosa in its bones. Whatever your assessment of these occurrences, take to heart, at least, the exhortations exemplified by Ben and Annetta to question everything, look past the surface, seek the truth, call out the people behind the curtain, and reject the social constructs that the "powers that be" use to herd and limit us.

When I finally braced myself to open the shoebox, I did so with naked fear.

Echoes may resound louder and more deeply than their source.

My awareness of the haunted world grows each time I work with Ben and Annetta.

So does its awareness of me. Dark paths upon which we tread lightly widen and branch to divert us from the brightness of accepted reality.

The story that follows is my effort to understand and explain all that happened that dark winter, to make sense of what I learned after I lifted the shoebox lid to expose a horrifying sight: a twelve-legged, spider-like creature the size of a grapefruit, its extra legs equipped with trident pincers, its many glittering eyes vaguely indigo. Countless, squirming hatchlings piled upon its back – hatchlings that erupted in dark streams that wriggled in every direction. Before I even thought of slapping the lid closed to contain them, they scurried and scattered everywhere, on my desk, down my legs, around my feet, onto the walls and ceiling, into my bookshelves – and then vanished into the creases and shadows of my office, taking up invisible residence, leaving behind the desiccated husk of their brood mother.

She crumbled to dust when I jostled the box.

Nothing more intruded into my life until several weeks later, when Ben called and invited me to meet with him and Annetta.

Their call, as I later learned, was not the one the voice ordered must be answered, and I was not the one to answer it, anyway. That dreadful duty fell to Ben and Annetta and a handful of ordinary people who experienced harrowing events that upended their ordinary lives. For the following account of that cold, gloomy season, their names have been changed to protect their privacy. Do not search them out. Seek to learn no more of them or what happened to them.

Believe me when I say that all you need to know of these matters is contained within these pages.

Anything not recorded here is either not worth knowing – or not worth the price of knowing.

James Chambers
Northport, NY

CHAPTER ONE

Summary of an audio recording made by Benjamin Keep interviewing Nestor Clemente, age 26, building engineer and assistant facilities manager, and Karina Clemente, age 23, artist and elementary school art teacher, recounting their experiences along the Ocean Parkway on November 28, Thanksgiving Day, around 11 P.M.; interview conducted December 6th.

Long Island's Ocean Parkway runs a little more than fifteen and half miles along a stretch of barrier island that comprises Jones Beach and Captree State Parks as well as several shore communities and private beaches. Built in the 1930s and listed on the National Register of Historic Places, it offers a scenic drive of Long Island's Great South Bay to the north and the Atlantic Ocean to the south. Lined by rolling dunes, lush beach grass, and coastal brush, it houses various wildlife, including even occasional winter sightings of the elusive snowy owl. In summer and good weather, traffic overflows it with the constant roar of sun-worshippers flocking to its beaches and boardwalk — but in winter and late at night, it offers a respite from Long Island traffic, a shortcut along the South Shore with connections to several northbound parkways. So desolate at times that for decades it served the infamous Long Island Serial Killer as a dumping ground for bodies.

Along this road, Nestor drove his Hyundai SUV with his wife, Karina, heading home to Babylon from Thanksgiving with Karina's family in Freeport, their first as a married couple. They had enjoyed the holiday and looked forward to relaxing the following Friday when they both had the day off. Heading south on the Meadowbrook Parkway, they merged onto the Ocean Parkway then turned east. As they approached a well-known local landmark, the Jones Beach Water Tower, nicknamed "the Pencil," Karina noticed something odd:

"The sky was so clear; you could see the stars perfect. The moon was just a sliver. You know, the little slice with the sharp points at either tip? So it was extra dark. The streetlights there barely light patches of the highway. I told Nestor to slow down. He likes to drive fast, and there are rarely cops down there, but there are deer and other animals to avoid. We were coming to the roundabout when I spotted the thing at the top of the Pencil. I've driven by it hundreds of times. It has always been just a big, sharp point in the sky, nothing else ever up there, which is why I noticed the thing. What would be there on Thanksgiving, right? It looked like four, jumbo-size, black trash bags, hanging off a scarecrow, flapping in the wind. Maybe a bunch of party balloons got loose, floated there and got snagged, I figured — except it had these red lights. You know, like to warn planes? When we drove into the roundabout, I lost sight of it until we came out the other side. When I saw the Pencil again, it was gone."

Karina told her husband what she saw. Tired and eager to get home, he shrugged it off, and the couple traveled along the parkway without another car in sight, unusual even for a holiday. Given the late hour, though, they thought little of it. Proceeding beyond the last of the Jones Beach Parking Fields, Nestor switched on his high-beams, wary of deer along the shoulder. He drove well above the speed limit, feeling as if he owned the road. Karina begged him to slow down. He conceded only a few miles per hour — until Karina screamed. Then he slammed on the brakes. She saw the thing in the road before he did. Her warning kept them from colliding with the broad, black shape suddenly spanning both eastbound lanes.

"I thought it was a roadblock," Nestor said. "Couple of sawhorses with tarps draped on them. Maybe an accident up ahead, right, but there were no flashing lights, nobody directing the traffic. Not that there was any, but it was still weird. We skidded, hell yeah. I was pushing eighty-five when Karina freaked. I kept it tight, though. She gets skittish if I go fast at night, but I know how to drive, trust me. I stopped fifteen feet from the blockade then inched forward. Right when our headlights lit up the blockade, it… well, the whole damn thing jumped into the sky, leaving the road open. Don't ask me how. I can imagine tarps blowing away but sawhorses too? It was like someone caught the whole mess with a giant fishing line then — *yoink* — snatched it out of sight."

"There was no wind that night, not even a breeze. It was the kind of night that's so still you want to sit out and stare at the sky, but it's just too cold," Karina said.

"I got out and looked around. There was nothing, not even litter. It was strange, man. The air felt heavy, like before a thunderstorm. You know? It hung in my mouth and throat and lungs. Damp, too. And I didn't hear a thing. No other cars, no planes, not even the waves. When it's that quiet, you hear waves rolling in from the Atlantic but, nope, not that night. The other messed-up thing? Our radio died. Karina insists on playing the Christmas station starting Thanksgiving, and it sputtered out right in the middle of Mariah Carey's 'All I Want for Christmas,' and thank god, because I already needed a break from that. Still damn strange, right? We started going again. I took it slow, just in case—at least until the thing chased us," Nestor said.

"We never saw where it came from, but it stomped on the car roof, made loud, whomping thumps, three in a row, *thump, thump, thump,* then gave a high-pitched screech, then three more thumps," Karina said. "Like it wanted to come through the roof."

"That's when I freaked," Nestor said. "I pictured a raccoon, a fox, or an owl, something with claws or talons, stuck up there, scratching up the paint. I mean, I'm still making payments on those wheels. So I jammed the brakes again, planning to get out and chase it off, but the thing up there lost its grip. It overshot the front hood and tumbled into the road. We almost hit it. Then it stood up in the headlights, and… damn it, man, I don't like to think about it. I wish I could unsee it. A thing like that shouldn't exist. Can't exist, right? It had to be a dream or… You know what? This is crazy. We said enough now. Turn that thing off. Stop recording us."

Following a pause in the recording, after which Nestor and Karina argued in whispers too low for their words to register, Ben prompted them to continue. Nestor, with an edge in his voice, reminded Ben he promised not to use their real names or to publicize them in any way, that they agreed to this to help themselves understand what they'd experienced and help Ben and Annetta with their research, which they believed concerned folk tales and nothing else. Despite Nestor's threatening tone, Ben confirmed their agreement.

"Okay, so, what I saw…" Karina said, "…was like several different creatures all at once. First, it looked like an eight-foot tall, hunchback man draped from head to toe in a long, black cloak and wearing a mask with glowing red eyes the size of dinner plates. It didn't move like a person. It rotated and twisted. That's when I saw its thin, bony body with a rippling feathery coat as the cloak spread like those flapping trash bags on the Pencil. The bags formed into wings. Not like a bat or a bird but definitely wings. Layered. Shimmering like... like moth wings, but with a scaly base. The thing rippled then became monstrous. Its body turned muscular. It sprouted claws from its fingers and toes. Its wingspan expanded until I couldn't see the road past it, not even the median or the shoulder. Its face turned bulbous. Its red eyes bulged. They glowed so bright I had to squint. It opened a mouth full of wriggling feelers and needle teeth. Its wings curved around us like arms reaching for a hug. It screeched. That sound ripped through me. Like when you're too close to a speaker at a concert, and a high note goes straight to your bone and muscle. It made my head spin."

Nestor, growing obviously uncomfortable with the interview, answered curtly when Ben asked if he saw the same things. "I saw something big, dark, weird, and loud. It made my skin crawl and hurt my head," he said. "Otherwise, all I'll say is my wife don't lie."

"Things got confusing," Karina said. "We stared at it for, I don't know how long, maybe seconds or minutes, maybe longer. I couldn't look away, couldn't speak. Like it'd hypnotized us. I managed to put my hand on Nestor's. He felt so cold I started crying. We couldn't move until the thing flapped its wings three times and lifted into the sky. As its feet left the light of the car's headlights, its hold on us ended. I shouted at Nestor to drive, to get us the hell out of there."

"It's the only time she didn't complain about me speeding," he said. "We hit ninety. The thing didn't go back on our roof, but it wasn't done with us."

"It followed us," Karina said. "Out the back windshield I saw it gliding over the road. Its wings stretched so far I couldn't see the tips of them. It changed as it moved, all the versions I'd seen of it blending into new combinations but never losing its basic shape — those massive wings and red eyes. It paced us until we neared the end of Ocean Parkway. We had to drive into Captree State Park, a dead end, or exit to the Robert Moses Causeway."

"I hit the exit, brakes screeching, tires squealing. The car almost lifted onto two wheels," Nestor said, stifling a dry, self-impressed laugh. "Not my best moment, no, but even I don't hit ninety on those off-ramp curves. I kept it frosty, though, you know I did, and merged onto the Robert Moses, and floored it north."

"It didn't stay with us," Karina said. "I closed my eyes when we hit the ramp, terrified of how fast Nestor was driving. When I looked again, it was gone. A few seconds later, the radio switched itself on. 'God Rest Ye Merry Gentleman' by the Bare-Naked Ladies, one of the only songs that Nestor likes on that station. It came back on the line, '…to save us all from Satan's power.' Now, that's not a coincidence, is it? What if the thing was the Devil or a demon and the song was a sign? An omen? You think it could've been? If not, what the hell was it? You have any idea?"

The recording continued with conversation as Ben admitted he had no answers to explain the weird encounter, but he doubted it was the "capital D" Devil. The line in the Christmas carol represented a "synchronicity," an unrelated event in which the universe sometimes echoes itself, lending significance to trivial details. Nestor and Karina responded in the negative when asked if they had experienced other strange occurrences, such as disembodied voices, lost time, visits by Men in Black, and so on. They claimed they'd never been interested in unusual phenomena, had in fact been lifelong skeptics of anything mystical outside the teachings of their church.

Thanking them, Ben concluded the interview by asking if either felt anything other than fear during their encounter.

"Anger," Nestor said. "That thing messed up my car and scared my wife."

After a moment of hesitation, Karina said, "When it screeched, I almost felt… like it wanted to warn us of something important. But we were only driving home. What the hell could it have wanted to warn us about?"

Chapter Two

Against my better judgement, we interviewed the Clementes because Annetta insisted on it. After returning from our "vacation" to Australia, we had achieved enough equilibrium to get married and move into my childhood home in Hicksville. Years we'd spent keeping a low profile and living in unlikely places had done nothing to shelter us from paranormal forces that invaded our lives, so we gave up trying to hide anymore. They would find us wherever we went. Why not take advantage of the home my folks had left me when they moved to Florida? With the housing market the way it is on Long Island, how could we not?

If the Amityville horror happened today, you think the Lutzes would flee a bargain like that? Not a chance. What do a ghost pig and blood dripping from the walls matter against the horror of a high-interest mortgage?

Annetta, who worked with Karina Clemente's older sister, Octavia Benitez, at King's College, wanted to do her friend a favor. Octavia knew about our work researching occurrences outside "normal" science. She didn't believe in anything she couldn't see in plain sight or under a microscope, but the Thanksgiving occurrence had left her sister and new brother-in-law rattled. She wanted Annetta to listen to them then give them a rational explanation. "Make some shit up if you have to," she'd said. "They just need to tell someone who won't laugh at them, you know? Get it out of their system. Then I won't have to listen to Kari go on and on about this nonsense anymore."

Annetta agreed to listen, but not to lie. Octavia arranged the meeting.

We spent four hours with the Clementes, during which I tried to poke holes in their story, highlight contradictions, and expose lies or fabricated memories. My efforts failed. By the end of our conversation, we achieved two things. One, the Clementes seemed genuinely relieved that we'd listened and didn't mock them. Two, they'd convinced us they'd experienced a genuine, paranormal event, the significance of which they remained ignorant, while it set every hair on my neck on end.

After they left, Annetta and I sat in silence for a long time, neither of us ready to voice the question burning in both our minds. Late afternoon sunlight streaming through the window painted bronze shadows on her deep brown skin.

Finally, I said: "Could they have really encountered the Mothman?"

A wide smile creased Annetta's lips. "Oh my god, I didn't want to be the one to say it, but it sure sounds like they did, doesn't it? What the hell is the Mothman doing on Long Island?"

"Don't jump the gun. We don't know what they really saw. Granted, they believe every word they told us. They saw something on that road, and it frightened them, and it sounds like the Mothman — but that particular cryptid has never been widely reported outside of West Virginia. So what on earth would it be doing on Long Island?"

"Until we found one living in the Peconic River, no one had ever reported a bunyip outside of Australia," Annetta said. "Cryptids get around. Maybe it's been here all along and no one saw it or said anything if they did."

"You never hear about Nessie making the rounds of the Scottish lochs," I said, but then I conceded her point.

In a strange quirk, the modern world — where more people than at any other time in history dismiss superstition and the supernatural, where a sizable portion of the population considers religion archaic — somehow offers as many if not more hiding places for mysterious things than the ancient world did. Yes, old maps labeled regions of land or sea with "Here Be Monsters," but today, anywhere you look you can pin a dozen obscure places with the same label: abandoned factories, hospitals, houses, schools, and shops; wild niches fenced off between the boundaries of suburban sprawl; vacant lots and historic cemeteries tucked beside strip mall parking lots; dark alleys and forgotten storefronts; undying, impenetrable shadows cast by tall buildings; miles and miles of underground tunnels of so many different kinds, no one knows them all.

The old world of monsters and mysteries never left. It merely adapted to new shadows in the spaces humanity created and forgot.

Annetta and I had resisted this fact in the past. To no avail, of course.

Once you set foot willingly across the boundary between accepted reality and the haunted world, once you peel back the curtain and peek at the inner workings of the universe, you can no longer deny that humanity lives in a bubble of so-called enlightenment we collectively choose not to pop for convenience's sake. Ever since researching the Montauk Monster, Annetta and I and some of our friends have walked the fine line between exploring and explaining that phantasmic world—and not bursting the bubble. Thus Annetta's excitement worried me.

A biologist and zoologist, she viewed everything through the lens of science, and science, like nature, abhors a vacuum. Or rather, scientists do. Scientists seek knowledge and explanation in a never-ending pursuit to study, refine, and improve humanity's understanding of the universe. A chance to investigate one of the most infamous cryptids in history left Annetta charged up and ready for a full-on investigation. On the other hand, I tried not to dampen her enthusiasm, but I feared any investigation would take us much deeper down whatever rabbit hole we unearthed than she imagined. They had before, even endangering our lives. Our survival to date seemed to make us the de facto contacts for beings from beyond in need of human agents to manipulate events in our world—or at least on Long Island. It sounds glamourous, sure, but the pay sucks, the hours are worse, and you'll never sleep well again.

Where Annetta rushed in, I dragged my feet. We balanced each other. I knew I'd never dissuade her from investigating, so instead, I tapped my memory of John Keel's classic, *The Mothman Prophecies*, a book I'd read many times and offered Annetta a rational if not obvious starting point.

"We should stakeout Mount Misery," I said.

"What? Why? Where's that? We should start on the Ocean Parkway," Annetta said.

"We should check it out at some point," I said, "but during the years when Mothman was first reported, in the months before and after the Silver Bridge collapsed, Mount Misery was the site of multiple Men in Black encounters. If the MIBs are pulling us back in, maybe we'll find them roaming around up there." The Men in Black had interfered in our encounters with the Montauk Monster and the Bunyip, guiding our research, watching us, or scaring the hell out of us.

"The Clementes said nothing about the Men in Black. If the MIBs are pulling us into some of their nonsense, they know where to find us without us looking for them. If we step on their toes, they'll let us know," Annetta said. "We start on the parkway."

I knew her tone of voice well enough not to argue any further

The next night I found myself driving west along the Ocean Parkway ten minutes after midnight, Annetta beside me, her infrared camera on her lap while she gazed out the window at the overcast night sky and the darkness along the highway's edges. Our fifth run of the night and we'd seen nothing but clouds and lonely cars, lights in the beach houses, and at the westernmost end of the highway near the terminus of the barrier island, the scintillant glow of a drive-through Christmas lights display that had opened at one of the beach parking fields. The lights reflected on the low clouds, painting that patch of sky in brilliant, flickering spots of green, red, yellow, blue, and gold. Perfect cover for a red-eyed creature to hover overhead and hide.

We reached the Pencil and the roundabout, drove full circle and headed east for another loop of the parkway. Annetta tapped her fingers against the top of her camera and said nothing. Her silence telegraphed her disappointment.

"It would be a miracle," I said, "if we came down here and spotted anything right off the bat. You know that, right? We've been out here a couple of hours. The original sightings of the Mothman were irregular. Conditions aren't the same as the night of the Clementes's encounter. That's assuming they didn't really see what Karina first thought: a bunch of garbage bags or balloons blowing around."

Gaze focused on the roadside, Annetta said, "You don't believe them?"

"I believe they told us the truth, but they were tired, and it was dark. There was tension over Nestor's driving, the kind of friction newlyweds might suppress or redirect to avoid a fight. How do we know they didn't just spook themselves into seeing more than was there?"

"We don't. But Karina's descriptions were so specific. How could she come up with that if she hadn't really seen it?"

"Everyone's heard of the Mothman," I said.

Annetta shifted in her seat, her finger-taps ceasing. "Really, everyone?"

"Yeah, there was that movie with Richard Gere. And plushies. They make Mothman toys and comic books. You can probably even buy Mothman fluffy slippers and stuff. Who doesn't at least have a picture of Mothman in their head when they hear the name? Karina had, like, three or four of them, all of which we've heard before, right? One sounded like the metal statue in Point Pleasant. That's pretty famous."

"She never called it Mothman, never said the name. We never said the name to her and Nestor," Annetta said.

"She probably never read the book, maybe never watched the movie, just saw the thing around and gleaned fragments that stuck in her memory. It's embedded in the cultural landscape. Everything's everywhere all the time, screaming at you from online ads, or social media, or store shelves, even in graffiti. No one remembers where they saw every odd, little thing that sticks in their head. Karina's an art teacher. I bet one of her students drew it. Kids love cryptids. I'm only saying we could be on a false trail here."

"I admit the possibility," Annetta said. "You want to go home?"

"Already?"

"Isn't that what you were trying to talk me into?"

"No. Just moderating our expectations. I'm game as long as you are."

"All right, one more circuit, then we'll call it a night."

I guided our car into the entrance to Captree State Park, turned around in the parking lot, and drove west again. The distant lights of the Christmas show winked out, the display closed for the night, ripping color from the charcoal sky as if a dozen stained-glass windows had shattered, and their fragments evaporated. For a heartbeat, I glimpsed two red lights in the gloom, but then more lights joined them as planes emerged from the clouds on approach to JFK and LaGuardia airports. We drove. Neither of us spoke as we waited for an increasingly unlikely answer to the question hanging over us. At the western end of Ocean Parkway, I routed east once more and commenced our last run along the path Nestor and Karina had followed, up the Robert Moses Causeway and home. We arced through the roundabout, passed the Pencil, every foot of road bringing us closer to the night's conclusion.

Ahead of us, maybe a mile, a light flared.

Brilliant, deep crimson, the rear lights of a high-end SUV, maybe.

Except as we neared it, the illumination expanded into a crimson dome tenting a patch of road and shoulder. Every instinct told me to stay away. Instead, I nudged the accelerator and sped toward the light. It swirled with smoke and mist. Its illumination reached ten feet or so from its source, limited to a circle that lit up so intensely everything within it turned absolute black or red. Tall shapes moved within the light. I stopped the car thirty feet away, too stunned to drive closer.

On the shoulder sat an unidentifiable, late model black sedan, its trunk open, red light flooding from the cargo space, rising from some deep nonsensical well or tunnel inside it. Fumes wafted up and turned the air hazy. By the left, rear driver's side of the car crouched two tall, thin men in black hats and long black coats over black suits, white shirts, and black ties. The car sat at an angle, jacked up on a heavy spring coil, a spare tire to one side, while one man loosened the lug nuts by spinning his index finger over them, not touching them, the steel whirling loose as if by magic. After a moment, both men looked at me and Annetta. The crimson blast rendered their pale, smooth faces featureless. One stood and waved for us to pass, smiling and tipping his hat. Helpless to do anything else, I put the car in drive and cruised onward, skirting the edge of the red light.

Annetta grabbed my right wrist and squeezed, sending her tension into me.

The scene dwindled in the rearview mirror until the Man in Black crouched and returned to helping the other with the tire—and then everything—the light, the car, the Men in Black—all simply winked out of existence, and darkness reclaimed the space they'd occupied.

Chapter Three

Summary of an audio recording made by Benjamin Keep interviewing Blanche Palmieri, age 56, a homemaker and interior decorator, and Hayley Palmieri, age 22, her daughter, recounting an overnight experience at their home in the Mount Misery area of Long Island; interview conducted December 22nd.

The Mount Misery area, which includes the highest elevation on Long Island, consists of winding roads, dense with trees and lined with high-end homes on large plots. It stands a few miles west of Sweet Hollow Road, itself home to a multitude of local urban legends. The two points mark the edges of an unusual zone. Passing through it, especially late at night or during bad weather, feels like dropping back to a primeval time.

While local folklore holds that ghosts haunt Sweet Hollow Road, they disagree on the history and origins of the phantasms. Some say a school bus full of children skidded off the icy Northern State Parkway overpass, crashing and killing all the passengers; if you park your car there at night, put it in neutral and wait, the invisible hands of dead children will push you out from under the plummeting bus. Others claim six teenagers hung themselves from the overpass, fulfilling a bizarre suicide pact with no known motive, the identities of the tragic teens unknown. Other stories speak of a lady in white, a classic folktale, who approaches cars at night and seeks a ride following a car crash in which she and her lover died. One version says she needs a ride to return to an influenza sanatorium from which she escaped only to get lost and die of disease and exposure. In perhaps the goriest tale, a police officer stops speeding cars, requests the driver's license, then turns back to his cruiser only to reveal the gory cavity of a gunshot wound that blew away the back and top of his head.

As dark and tragic as those stories are, they fall short of the sheer weirdness reported on Mount Misery. To this day, a nineteenth-century burial ground remains along that road, its forgotten graves stretching into the hills. Rumors linger about another sanitarium that once stood there but burned to the ground in some past century, claiming the lives of all its occupants. Rumors linger… about a secret military base devoted to psychotropic experiments, part of MKUltra; about Native Americans who believed the land toxic, home to the Thunderbird; about silent, odd lights hanging in the night sky above the hills and trees — and of encounters with Men in Black.

"I never would've opened the door that late, but I thought it was Hayley's ex-boyfriend. He won't leave her alone. Ever since she's home from rehab, he calls five, six times a day, even drives by the house," Blanche said. "I run interference for her, because that loser's still using. He wants to pick things up with Hayley right where he left them, but she's clean, and she's going to stay that way. If that dirtbag thinks he'll get his hooks back into her, he's in for a rude lesson. Okay, right, right, sorry, I'm going on a tangent, but that's why I opened the door after midnight. I wanted to tell the bum off. Yes, I should've hit the panic button on our home security system, not that it would've done a whole lot of good. The damn thing doesn't even work, but — yes, sorry, sorry. Okay, so what I expected when I opened the door was a skinny kid in torn jeans and a black leather jacket who looks like he weighs eighty pounds soaking wet and has the worst damn complexion I've ever seen on a man, and I use that term loosely when I'm talking about Garth. The only thing that boy changes is which stained T-shirt he has on and how long his hair is. What I got was a man at least six foot five, dressed in a black suit, black overcoat, black wide-brimmed hat, and my first impression was he was Amish. I even looked past him for the horse and buggy. It made no sense! Well, maybe more sense than what he turned out to be. The cold swept in, and I shivered. Hayley hung around in the hall behind me, trying to catch a glimpse of Garth."

"What about his face, Mom," Hayley said. "He was pale, like he was wearing powder make-up. His features were like a baby's, like they weren't all the way formed yet. Like he didn't have control of his expressions. He looked all angry and mean saying something polite, and then when he got mad, he smiled. Like that."

Blanche confirmed this then clearing throats and the slurping sounds of people drinking coffee or tea filled the recording as Ben and Annetta gave the Palmieri's time to collect their thoughts.

"I asked him what he wanted. He smiled. He opened his mouth a couple of times like he was about to say something, but he didn't. I looked past him again, not for a buggy, but worried he had friends with him. I didn't see anyone. But that's not all I didn't see. Our front walkway glistened in the glow of the lamppost at the entrance and the porchlight by the door. Rain turned the spaces around the flagstones into a muddy mess. It always does. But there wasn't a single footprint, not in the mud, not on the flagstones. Okay? Every time we get more than a drizzle; our front walk looks terrible. The mud gets all squished up. Dirty footsteps dry on the stones after the rain ends. It looks like hell until the landscapers come and sweep it tidy. You see what I'm saying?"

Ben said: "How did he get to the door? Where did he come from?"

"Exactly," Blanche said. "I'm standing there with the door open, cold air rushing in, this guy flapping his lips like a fish out of water, and fear is creeping into my mind. My husband, Roger, was away on business. It was me and Hayley home by ourselves. Now this guy shows up, and what the hell does he want? Where'd he come from? I start to close the door, but he shoves a foot in to block it, then frowns, and says, 'Oh, yes, I remember. You see, my car broke down on the road that goes by your house. May I use your phone to call for assistance?' He took his foot out of the door, rocked back on his heels, like a kid all happy and proud, but he's still frowning."

"Yeah, that's what I mean," Hayley interjected. "Like his brain forgot to tell his face he was supposed to be pleased with himself."

"I told him no way was he coming in, but if he told me his license plate number, I'd call roadside assistance for him. He didn't like that. He grinned and set me shivering again. Then he says, 'That's not neighborly of you. Don't you know how to help a person in need of assistance? How can you leave me stranded in the cold in a broken car? Now, let me use your phone. We'll forgive this little lapse and go back to being good neighbors. I'll forget what you told Benjamin Keep too. It's only a local call. Let me in. We'll talk about the things you said to Ben while we wait.' I don't know why he mentioned your name. I never heard of you before and not after until I looked you up online. I asked him didn't he have a cellphone, and he got all weird and puzzled, then he said, "Oh, right, my phone has no charge left. Sorry' He looked past my shoulder, and said to my daughter, 'Hayley, you'll let me in won't you? For a quick phone call? That's all. I promise. Be a good neighbor, won't you?'"

"I don't know how the hell he knew my name," Hayley said. "I didn't recognize him. He didn't look like anyone my old friends knew. I thought maybe Garth sent him to frighten me, but that's not Garth's style. He gets in your face and throws a tantrum."

"I shoved the door closed as far as I could," Blanche said. "He blocked it again with his foot. I asked Hayley if she knew him. She said she didn't, and I believed her. I saw in her eyes how frightened she was. I told her, call the police, then all of sudden, the door slammed shut. The man was gone. I checked the front path, still no footsteps, checked either side of the door, no one there. So I locked it then hit the security system panic button."

"I tried to call 911 on my phone," Hayley said. "I mean, I know, like the guy didn't try to force his way in or threaten us, but he really weirded me out."

"We're supposed to get a phone call within thirty seconds of hitting the button," Blanche said. "The phone rang once, started to ring again, but it went dead mid-ring. I answered it anyway and heard so much static, I couldn't make out anyone talking on the other end."

"My call failed. I tried it again and again. It kept ending before it went through, like there was no signal, but I had five bars, and I was on wi-fi. It should've worked."

"Same with my phone," Blanche said.

"Then he knocked at the back door," Hayley said.

"I looked out the kitchen window. It's the same guy. He waved and frowned. Then he vanished again. Knocking came from the front door for a few seconds, then someone pounded on the garage door. It's attached to the house, and it connects to the kitchen. Minutes passed, and I'm hoping the alarm company has sent someone to check on us. That's what they're supposed to do when they call and don't get the codeword. The codeword means everything's okay. If they don't hear it, they're supposed to send help. But time is passing. Now there's knocking coming from every door. There's tapping at all the windows, I can't even see who all is out there because it's so dark and the rain picked up, coming in heavy sheets. Hayley and I crouched behind the island in the kitchen, frightened to let them see us. I figure there's a whole group out there now, must be, right? A gang, I'm thinking, picturing every worst home invasion nightmare as shadows rush past the windows. I'm counting half a dozen or more people banging on our house, maybe more," Blanche said.

"They talked to us too," Hayley said. "I couldn't understand most of it. Their voices were too faint, or they talked too fast, but when I caught something, it sounded like the first guy. Their car broke down. Could they use the phone. We should watch what we say to Benjamin Keep. We should help them out. Didn't we know how to be good neighbors. Stuff like that."

"It went on for almost an hour," Blanche said.

"Then all at once it stopped," Hayley said. "No more knocking. No more talking."

"We waited a while before we came out from behind the island. No one was at the doors or windows. No one was around the house as far as we could see. Especially no cops and no one from the security service, fat lot of good all the money I pay every month does," Blanche said. "I hit the panic button again. The phone rang. I answered. This time I could hear a man on the other side. He asked me if the control panel had malfunctioned again. What do you mean 'again,' I asked, and he said he'd called me an hour ago. I'd given him the codeword, said the panel was glitching, and asked them to send someone to check it first thing in the morning. Oh, no, I most definitely did not, I said, but he insisted, said he even had it recorded. I argued some more, then I gave up. I didn't know what to think. Still don't. The system malfunctioning and our cell service crapping out, I can see those things happening at the worst time possible, as unlikely as it is, but a whole conversation I don't remember a single word of? Where I lied to the person who could help me? No. That just didn't happen."

"I called 911 then, and it went right through," Hayley said. "They wouldn't send anyone until morning, though, because... well, I sounded kind of crazy when I told them what happened, and... um, they kind of know me? They came out to our house a lot before I went to rehab. I said a lot of weird shit back then. Once I lied to them about another girl dealing drugs, so they'd arrest her because she flirted with Garth. So, they don't take me seriously. They wouldn't listen any better when I put my mom on the line because she used to give them a hard time when they hassled me. They said if the man knocking on the door was gone, there wasn't anything they could do. He'd gone to the next house down the block to find someone who'd help him call assistance, that's all. Call if he came back."

"He did come back, but we couldn't call," Blanche said.

"Neither of us wanted to sleep," Hayley said. "We were too shaken up. We watched old reruns of *Friends* and sat up, drinking coffee to stay awake. It didn't work. We both nodded off at some point, then I woke up screaming. I'd been dreaming of a giant black shadow with huge red eyes that glided through the sky when the man from the front door bumped into me. I opened my eyes. He was sitting next to me on the sofa. So close I could smell his breath. Wintergreen and hot dust. He patted my knee twice then asked if he could use the phone. I screamed and jumped back. Fell right over the arm of the sofa to the floor. When I got up, my mom was awake, asking me what was wrong. The man wasn't on the sofa anymore. He stood behind my mom, tipping his hat. I couldn't say a thing. I was too afraid. I pointed at him. My mom looked—but he vanished."

"We saw him five or six more times that night," Blanche said. "We didn't sleep again, oh, no. He'd show up in the kitchen, or at the end of the hallway to the bathroom or outside staring through a window. I even saw him peeping in through the window at the top of our stairs to the second floor. We never saw him at the same time. One of us spotted him, said something, then he disappeared before the other could see. He didn't say anything new, just about his broken-down car, or how we needed to be good neighbors, or be careful what we said to Benjamin Keep. He'd tip his hat, frown or smile, both expressions equally ugly. By dawn our nerves were shot, and we were jumping at any creak or shadow. Once the sun came up we didn't see him again and haven't seen him since. The alarm tech came later that morning and said there was nothing wrong with our panel. He kept it professional, but I could tell he thought we were lying. The cops came at noon, walked around outside, checked all the door locks, said they saw no sign of anyone having prowled outside, no indication of attempted or forced entry."

"The officers wouldn't listen to anything I had to say," Hayley said. "They stuck to my mom and hinted she was caught up in whatever hallucination I'd had, maybe they let me out of rehab too soon. They didn't even take notes."

"The man hasn't come back since," Blanche said. "Still, we're giving serious thought to moving. Unless you can tell us what the hell happened and how to make sure it never does again. Can you do that? I researched you before I called you, Mr. Keep. You've got a good reputation, as much as anyone can have online these days. I don't believe in the stuff you think is real. After that night, though, I've got an open mind." Blanche laughed without humor. "Oh, yeah, you can bet on that. I have to or I might lose my mind all together."

Chapter Four

Annetta and I left the Palmieris's house around dusk on the evening of December 22, having captured the details of their encounter but having failed to reassure them they'd seen the last of their Man—or Men—in Black. I stopped short of telling Blanche that once you see them, you're forever prone to seeing them, or at least noticing them, and they tend to make multiple visits before concluding their inexplicable business. Maybe she and her daughter would buck tradition.

"Never heard of a Man in Black behaving like that," Annetta said.

I pulled away from the curb and drove south out of the Mount Misery neighborhood toward Old Country Road. Surrounding houses, trees, and powerlines cut black angles and lines in all directions against the fading orange sky. Twilight brings the deepest shadows, when the setting sun sheds enough light to see by but too little for details to persist, as if it erases part of the world and rewrites it for the night. We passed the overgrown remnants of the two-hundred-year or older Colyer burial ground, the weatherworn green-and-white street sign that commemorated it nearly invisible in the gloom and overgrown by creeping vines. East along the wooded road, rolling in silence, because I didn't know what to make of Annetta's observation. No Man in Black had ever acted that way, no, but the incident set me to thinking of the Hopkinsville Goblins. In 1955 a Kentucky family reported short alien creatures laying siege to their farmhouse, terrorizing them through the night, clamoring at the windows, banging on the roof, watching them from the trees. I couldn't imagine a connection, but then what connection existed between Long Island and West Virginia to bring the Mothman here? What connection could I have imagined between Peconic Lake on Long Island and a forgotten billabong in the Australian Outback before Annetta and I found it for ourselves.

Recognizing my mood, Annetta let silence prevail, until I said, "I'm hungry."

"I could eat," she said.

"There's a diner up the road on 110," I said.

We parked in the half-full lot, ate in a quiet booth, the diner like every other diner on Long Island, but a little drabber and a little less comforting in the way diners sometimes feel like a refuge. Still, it served us fine. We ordered cheeseburgers deluxe and coffee. Outside the windows, traffic raced along six lanes of Route 110, workers speeding home as rush hour drew to a close, delivery trucks wrapping up the last of their routes, people heading to eat dinner, or go shopping, or meet their dates, or any of the infinite possibilities that guaranteed the flow of cars never ceased. I ate half my cheeseburger and started my second cup of coffee, before I sat back, and said, "Why the hell did they mention me?"

Annetta daubed her lips with her napkin. "We're are not exactly strangers to these folks, whatever or whoever they are."

"Okay, yeah, we've had our run-ins, and because of that we know they aren't shy about letting us see them," I said. "So why not come right to us? Why drop my name to a couple of scared women and hope they'll look me up, that I'll even answer if they call."

"They did call, and you answered," she said. "Manipulation is part of their game isn't it? They put their fingers on the scales and shift the balance. They don't give orders."

"True," I said. "Or maybe they have to do it that way."

"What does that mean?"

"That they can't interfere. They can't act firsthand. They're allowed to put ideas into the wind like seeds and see where they take root. They frighten people to… to fertilize or nurture those ideas, make sure they aren't forgotten."

"Allowed by who? Or what? The Department of Weird Shit?"

"Ha-ha. No idea. Something higher up in the cosmic order doing the same thing to them."

"Hah! You mean Men in Black that mess with the Men in Black? Sure, I can buy that. It's no stranger than anything else we've considered. You think they wanted us to go to the Palmieris's house?"

"I think they wanted us to visit Mount Misery."

"Oh, no, you are *not* going to 'told you so' me on this one. Staking out Ocean Parkway was a reasonable move, and we did experience something that night."

"Which meant what? What the hell did we even see? Since when do the Men in Black's cars get flats? I didn't even think those things were entirely — I don't know — *physical*. You ever see one of their vehicles show so much as a scratch, let alone mechanical failure?"

"I never thought about it. The way they come and go, make no sound, vanish, yeah, it's like a ghost car. But we don't see them all that often. For all we know, they take their cars to a garage on the Moon every night for repair and cleaning."

"Yeah, maybe," I said around a French fry before chewing and swallowing. "The moon? Really? You think they're set up on the moon."

Annetta kicked me under the table. "You know what I mean."

"Okay, but what if that's part of the message? The failure, the break down."

"The MIB who came to the Palmieris's said his car broke down."

"Exactly."

"That's the lore, though. They make up mundane-sounding excuses for where they are."

"Yeah, yeah, but there's a thread there, right? Breakdowns."

"How does it help us?"

"I don't know. Maybe it doesn't. Maybe we have to pull more of the thread to unravel it."

After our meal, we left the diner restless from too much mystery and too much coffee. I exited the parking lot headed back the way we'd come, the opposite direction of the way home. Annetta noticed right away.

"What've you got in mind?" she said.

"A little night driving," I said. "Let's cruise the neighborhood. These things happen in clusters sometimes. We might get lucky."

"I should've gotten a coffee to go," she said.

"Then you'd wind up using a gas station bathroom later."

Annetta shivered. "True."

I drove west on Old Country Road back to Mt. Misery Road and as far up into the hills as the winding side street took us. It dead-ended at a claustrophobic cul-de-sac with a nursery school on one side and an enormous radio tower on the other, a primary broadcasting point for one of Long Island's local radio stations. Trees, shadows, and houselights glittering through skeletal branches and thick evergreen shrubbery formed terrestrial constellations. We turned back and roamed until reaching the intersection of Old Country Road and Sweet Hollow Road, the most haunted patch of pavement on Long Island. I drove north toward the infamous Northern State Parkway overpass. First, houses, then a cemetery, rolled by before the landscape gave way to the woods of the West Hills Preserve. Soon we approached a wall of darkness that inhabited the space below the stone arch of the overpass.

"No streetlights under there," Annetta said.

"Yeah, it's pitch black," I said, slowing the car.

A light glimmered in the dense black space, flickered, then extinguished.

"Is someone under there? Why's it so dark?" Annetta said.

"It shouldn't be, right? It's not that dark out tonight. The space below the overpass isn't that wide, maybe sixty feet, just enough for four lanes of parkway."

"It's like there's a curtain hanging from the top. What do we do?"

"Drive through like we planned."

"You sure?"

"You know how many kids goof around on this stretch of road? You ever hear of anything actually happening to them? We'll be fine."

I nudged the accelerator and entered the darkness. The sense of light slipped away as we pulled beneath the overpass, then visibility abruptly improved under the stone arch, and the road on the far side grayed deeper into shadow. A parked car sat on the southbound shoulder. Its driver's door hung open. Its dome light off or dead, the interior remained draped in darkness. We passed it in seconds then left the overpass. I turned around at the next intersection then stopped near a patch of woods.

"Something felt wrong under there," I said.

"Wrong how? Stupid kids messing around in the dark wrong?"

"No. Did you feel like we should've been able to see better under there? Like something blacked out things in our view?"

Annetta's expression said no. "It's dark. The car light is busted. Or they turned it off to enhance the mood. Maybe the bulb just died."

"Let's go back," I said.

"Okay, sure, let's do that," said Annetta.

As we neared the overpass, I lowered my window. Icy air flooded the car. Annetta made a shivery sound but didn't protest. I slowed as we passed the parked car. Then stopped. The oddity of the total absence of other traffic struck me then. Only a two-lane avenue, Sweet Hollow Road still saw plenty of traffic as a backway to cut north from 110 to Route 25 and duck a lot of traffic and stoplights. Cars traveled it regularly day and night. We hadn't seen another vehicle besides the one parked beneath the overpass since I'd turned off Old Country Road.

As if reading my mind, Annetta popped open the glove compartment and grabbed my flashlight. She switched it on, lowered the passenger window, and lit up the parked car as more cold air flowed in around us. Empty. The passenger doors, front and back, hung open too. As if driver and passengers had fled the car, not caring about securing it.

I pulled ahead of the abandoned car and parked on the shoulder outside the stone base of the overpass. We exited and let the flashlight beam lead us to the abandoned car. We poked our heads inside, saw nothing unusual, unless being uncluttered and clean counts. Starbucks cups occupied cup holders, front and back, wafting the lingering aroma of cinnamon. I reached below the steering wheel, popped the trunk, and then took a look. Empty except for old blankets, a case of bottled water, and a roadside emergency kit. We scanned the shoulder to the woods but saw nothing of interest.

"Let's say the car broke down, and they left," Annetta said.

"Leaving all the doors open?"

"It was a dare. They all ran into the woods," she said. "Something blew out the window. They all went chasing it."

"Yeah, sure, maybe," I said. "A for effort, hon."

"We can report it to the police. There's not much else we can do about someone leaving their car on the shoulder. It's not even a no-parking zone."

I sighed. "Yeah, you're right. Let's get out of here. It's cold."

My hand on the driver's side door handle, I froze at the sound of a voice calling from up the gentle slope of the dark woods. Amidst the trees, nothing but layers of shadow and the faint haze of a mounting fog. When I'd convinced myself I'd imagined it, the voice called again: *It's a light! Follow the light!*

A woman's voice, faint, distorted by the breeze, and the rustle of dead leaves. Annetta heard it too. She aimed the flashlight up the hill, into the woods, searching, scanning.

It's brighter, see? Go that way!

The voice again. As if cotton balls fell from my ears, sound surged at me.

I hadn't realized how the density of the darkness beneath the underpass dimmed sound as well as sight. Now dry leaves and sticks crunched under footsteps with the sharpness of breaking bones. Bodies moved among gnarled tree trunks.

"This way, here!" the woman called, her voice crisp and clear now.

She and two others emerged from among the trees into the flashlight glow.

"Help us! Please, help!" she cried when she saw us.

The trio skidded down the gentle incline. The woman wore a ski jacket, leggings, and winter ankle boots, her brown hair pulled back in a long ponytail. Behind her came a man in a long, gray overcoat and a black knit cap, holding the hand of another woman, wearing a downy, purple coat that fell below her knees and clung to her figure. Bits of leaves and twigs bobbed in her long, black hair.

"What happened?" I said. "Are you lost?"

"Aaron is still in there. He can't find his way back. I think *it* got him. Please, help us find him," the first woman said. "My name is Bronwyn. This is Eddie and Gina. We stopped to see if the ghosts would really push our car. They didn't, and we were going to leave, but then Aaron's car wouldn't start, okay? And then… something… I don't know what, freaked him out, and he ran into the woods. We went after him, but we got lost, and it's so dark in there."

"It's more than dark," Eddie said. "It's fucking weird, like… I don't know, man, like the ground changes while you're walking on it."

"What's the 'it' you said got your friend?" I asked.

"I don't know, oh, god, but it's fucking big. It has black wings and red eyes. It dropped out of the trees, right onto Aaron, then we couldn't see him anymore, and we couldn't see our way back to the road, not until we saw your light. *Please* help us."

Annetta and I exchanged glances, silently agreeing.

"All right," I said. "We're going to need more light."

Chapter Five

We took four road flares from the kit in Aaron's trunk and my flashlight. Bronwyn guided us into the woods where they'd last seen Aaron. Annetta walked behind her to keep us from getting separated. Eddie and Gina stayed by the cars with two of the road flares and instructions to light one if we didn't return in fifteen minutes. If we didn't show by the time the first flare burned out, they were to light the second, take my car, and get help.

Deadfall crunched underfoot. Pebbles and stones rattled down the slight incline.

We marched on, deeper into whorls of darkness gathered among leafless trees, and in less than two minutes lost all awareness of the nearby road, all sense of orientation. Darkness draped behind us like a velvet curtain strung between tree trunks. Looking to the sky, the stars appeared dim and more distant than I'd ever seen them.

"Stop," I said.

"What? What is it?" Bronwyn said. "We have to keep moving. We have to find Aaron."

"We will but look and listen. This doesn't feel right," I said.

Annetta cupped her hands to her mouth and cried out, "Eddie! Gina! Can you hear me?"

I placed a finger to my lips to silence Bronwyn when I saw her about to speak. We waited thirty seconds, no reply. Annetta called out once more. Again, no answer.

"They should hear me. We're not that far," she said.

"Yeah, it's like the dark beneath the overpass. It's muting light and sound. We should be able to see farther back the way we came too. It's like that ground has been wiped away," I said.

"What the hell are you talking about?" Bronwyn's voice rattled with near hysteria and urgency. "Are we lost? Oh my god! We have to find Aaron. You're supposed to be helping. How can you help if you're already lost?"

"We're not lost," I said. "I promise you that. Think about it. We're on Long Island. How lost can you get when you can pick a direction and keep going until you hit water, right? And we won't even have to go that far if we do lose our way. Major roads run along every border of these woods. Fifteen, twenty minutes walking tops, we'll know where we are."

"Then what the fuck are you saying?" Bronwyn said.

I explained what Annetta and I had experienced beneath the overpass, how we heard her voice from the woods, dim and stifled at first, before they saw our light. "Whatever caused that is following us — or not following exactly but centered on us. Moving where we go. It's what made it seem to Eddie that the ground shifted underfoot. It's probably why you lost Aaron in the first place. Whatever this weird dark effect is probably hid him from you."

Bronwyn gaped at me in confusion. Her lips trembled. Tears welled in her eyes.

"Honey," Annetta said to her. "Watch this."

She crouched and scrabbled around until she came up with a stone the size of a baseball. She hurled it into the veil of darkness behind us. The moment it reached the border between the immediate gloom and that thick pall of black, it winked out of existence. We never heard it hit the ground.

"Think of it like a bubble we're in," Annetta said. "I know how weird that is, trust me, but we're safe right here. I can't explain why it's happening, but it's not threatening. Don't you think we'd feel it if it was? Feel a sense of menace? But I don't, not at all. Do you?" She waited for Bronwyn to slowly shake her head, no. "Right, so it's here for other reasons. The only way we'll find Aaron is if we roll with it, keep cool, and stay smart. Can you do that? This is all new to you, I know. Part of your brain is screaming at you to panic and run. That won't help. Got it? Stick with me and Ben. We've been down paths like this before. We good?"

Bronwyn sniffled, took several deep breaths to compose herself, then nodded. "Yeah, we good."

"All right," I said. "Look around slowly. There's a gray spot in the dark." I pointed in a direction I believed to be west where the black curtain seemed faded and thin. "That's where we go. These phenomena tend to herd us in a direction. There's not much to gain by resisting it. Go with the flow. It will take us where we need to be."

Several steps toward the gray patch set us onto a proper trail, which led in our direction, deeper into the West Hills Nature Preserve, part of West Hills County Park. I had hiked these woods, but never at night, and never under the watch of whatever forces lingered around us now. As we progressed along the trail the gray zone lightened until it resolved into a gauzy mist that sparkled and reflected the flashlight beam into our eyes. Annetta angled the light down to avoid blinding us. A frigid, wet sensation blanketed me as we entered the mist. Bronwyn and Annetta, both shivering, felt it too.

"It's okay, Bronwyn. I promise. Stay close, keep cool, okay?" I said.

"Yeah, fine, just keep fucking moving so we don't spend more time than we need to here because this is really fucking strange, and I don't like it, and I'm worried about Aaron, okay?" She spoke through chattering teeth, struggling to keep her composure.

"You got it, let's go," I said.

We pushed through the mist until it thickened to an ephemeral, intangible, white webbing that broke into clutching, undulating strands where it touched us. The cold deepened and probed through my winter coat, my sweater, my shirt, and my flesh to stab icicles into my bones. Ten, fifteen, twenty more yards we walked—then a light beckoned to us. A hazy red shimmer hanging in midair. The mist dwindled as we approached it. The freezing sensation lifted, permitting body heat to restore itself, trickling back to my fingers and toes. A thick oak trunk stood between us and the light source, splitting it to either side in fans of crimson rays. Bronwyn and Annetta still with me, I rounded the trunk to a clearing bloated with a red dome of luminescence like the one Annetta and I'd seen on the Ocean Parkway. This time, though, no car, no road, no Men in Black. Instead, a scene that drove spikes of horror into my heart and sent waves of unprecedented terror through my brain confronted us. I almost screamed. I don't know how Annetta and, especially, Bronwyn, who lacked the same experience we had, controlled their own reactions. Maybe they didn't. Maybe they screamed, and their voices never reached my ears.

A young man, Aaron, I presumed, lay spread-eagle on his back in the clearing's center, his head elevated on a pile of dead, sodden leaves. His fingers dug and scratched at the earth in spasms, and his feet quivered, as if he were trying to run in a dream. His eyes gaped wide open, rolled back to their whites, which the intensity of the crimson glow turned into brimming pools of blood, as if they might overflow and run down his cheeks. Behind him loomed a massive, dark shape that challenged my brain to make sense of it. When I looked directly at it, pain exploded in my head, so I peeked at it again and again, stealing glances out of the side of my eye, stitching together a patchwork sense of a thin, ragged body, like bundles of twigs twined together with an overly large head sprouting from the neck, the receptacle for two giant, red multifaceted eyes from which the red light emanated. Wings arced to either side of it, sprouted from its shoulders, scintillant and rippling, webbed with dense and stifling black lines like the curtain of darkness that had trailed us into the woods. The thing stood more than eight feet tall, maybe as much as twelve, its height difficult to estimate because wings and body blended together in uncertain configurations. It hunched over Aaron. Its mouth hung open, a yawning oval from which dangled a feathery proboscis that snaked the length of its body and more, its terminus embedded in the top of Aaron's head.

The thing noticed our intrusion and flicked its stare in our direction. The totality of the red light cast by its eyes struck us with physical force. I staggered, tripped over a tree root, and toppled to the ground. My eyes seared from the blast, I scrambled onto my hands and knees, then back to my feet, calling for Annetta and Bronwyn. I no longer saw them or much of anything else besides the afterimage of the creature's silhouette printed in stark black and red on my retinas. I clamped my eyes shut, pressed the heels of my hands against them, as if to rub away the sensory memory, but the red still penetrated, revealing my finger bones like an X-ray picture.

I hollered for Annetta and Bronwyn. No answer.

I could barely hear my own voice inside my head. A dreadful hum filled my ears: the raw vibration of the cosmos. The grind and shake of the cogwheels, levers, and switches of reality, the machinery of the universe. Sound never meant for human ears. It bled through invisible cracks in existence and overwhelmed my senses. It wiped away what I considered the real world, the tangible earth beneath my feet, the cold air that filled my lungs. I floated, lifted and spun by the din, set adrift on a black current of raw energy flowing beneath the surface of the universe. The red faded from my eyes. Darkness and oblivion replaced it. Then tiny sparks of gold flared, like fireworks showers. They lasted for less than a second at a time, and soon they ceased. Full dark returned. I lost all sense of my body, felt no air coming into my lungs or leaving them, felt as if my heart had stopped beating, not forever, no, but as if I were trapped between heartbeats. My sense of time withered. This could've been for a millisecond or an eternity, and then—all together—like a dam bursting, awareness and reality gushed back to me.

I tasted dirt. Dry leaves clung to my lips, my face.

Cold air pressed against my back, cold earth against my chest.

A woman's voice screamed, wordless, full of terror, scream after scream until the sound turned raw and strained. I rolled onto my back. Leafless branches formed a tattered canopy. Stars filled the clear night sky.

"Annetta," I said.

No answer, but I knew the screams weren't hers.

I rose to my knees. In the clearing, Aaron lay unmoving on the ground. The creature and its red light were gone. Bronwyn knelt a few yards away from him, hands clutched to her ears, her eyes shut tight, her teeth bared, lips strained with her screams. Beside her, Annetta slumped against a tree trunk. I forced myself up and rushed to her, jostling her, afraid she'd never open her eyes, never speak again, never hold me in her arms, or sigh as I pressed my lips to hers to kiss her— then she moaned and shrugged as if shaking off a chill. Her eyelids fluttered then opened, and her gaze settled on me.

"What the hell was that?" she said.

Then she, too, heard Bronwyn's screams, and we hurried to her. Slowly, soothingly, we eased Bronwyn out of her panic, persuaded her to lower her hands and listen to us, to open her eyes and see the clearing, to refocus on helping Aaron. That resonated for her, and she crawled to him, helped him sit up as he recovered by degrees from whatever the creature had done to him. Of all of us, he seemed the least rattled.

When he regained awareness and caught his breath, he asked, "What happened? I think I tripped and fell. Hit my head. How long have I been out like this?"

Bronwyn didn't answer. Instead she pulled him tight to her and kissed him.

"We should get out of here," Annetta said. "Which way is back?"

"That way."

I pointed to a shaky red light in the distance, the glow of a road flare.

Chapter Six

Transcript of an audio recording made by Benjamin Keep interviewing Bronwyn Norris, veterinary office receptionist, age 22; Aaron Reynolds, bank loan officer, age 29, Eddie Gauthier, assistant manager, retail store, age 24; and Gina Puglisi, car dealership sales assistant, age 25, recounting their experience on Sweet Hollow Road and in the West Hills Preserve on the evening of December 22; interview conducted December 23.

Benjamin Keep: Let's keep this simple. Don't worry about anything you say being too wild or outlandish. Annetta and I were there with you, so you know we're not going to doubt or mock you. Besides, we've seen a lot more phenomena like this than you have, and we hope to help you make sense of what happened. Let it all out. Your impressions, your memories, no matter how wacky they sound, okay? Who'd like to start?

Gina Puglisi: We never should've been out there that night. I didn't want to go. It was cold and dark, and I didn't understand why we couldn't go do something normal like catch a movie or go out for a few drinks or dancing. I can't believe you all made me do that! Especially you, Eddie.

Eddie Gauthier: Gina, please, I'm sorry! How many times can I say it? None of us thought anything would really happen, okay? We figured it would be a laugh, a dumb story to tell at parties. If we'd known…

BK: Let's try to stick to what happened that night, okay? I sympathize with you, Gina, but think of this as a documentary. We need to record your experience in as much detail as possible so we can study it.

GP: Ugh, fine.

Bronwyn Norris: I suggested it. I'd heard the stories growing up. I always wanted to try it. Kids in my high school did it all the time, but none of my friends would go with me. I was too chicken to go by myself. We were sitting around bored, and—no offense, Gina—I didn't want to spend another night at the movies or hanging out in a bar. Same old, same old, you know? Like Eddie said, I thought it would be a good story to tell.

Aaron Reynolds: I went along because Bronwyn asked me. I didn't expect anything to really happen. I laughed when she told me the stories about that road, that parkway overpass. Shit, man, I mean they're only stories. Urban legends. I heard some of the same ones growing up in Pennsylvania. I always laughed them off. Why waste time on nonsense, right?

BK: You still feel the same way after that night?

AR: Yeah, man. Why wouldn't I? None of that stuff is real.

BK: How much do you remember of what happened?

AR: It's blurry, yeah, I mean, kind of mixed up because I hit my head. We went out there, parked the car, sat and waited. We got bored when nothing happened. We wandered into the woods. I don't remember why. I fell, knocked myself out, and you guys found me.

[Note: Aaron spent a night in the hospital during which doctors determined that while he might have hit his head hard enough to stun him, he did not have a concussion. They noted a laceration on the back of his skull with swelling and bruising, likely from where he struck a rock, a branch, or a root, coincidentally in the same spot where the creature's probiscis appeared attached to his scalp. Bronwyn chose not to share anything out of the ordinary with his doctors.]

BK: That's it? So, why do you think you went into the woods?

AR: I don't know. I don't remember that. Why did we go into the woods, Bron?

BN: We followed you, Aaron. You took off running into the trees. We chased you. Why did you do that? You freaked out in the car, shouted about something coming after you then you bolted. What the hell was that about?

AR: No, way. That didn't happen. I'd remember that.

EG: Yeah, it totally happened, dude. We were talking about getting out of there when you lost your shit. We thought you were having a seizure or something. You shouted "It's coming. It's almost here. It's after me." Then, bang, you shot out of the car and ran.

BK: Let's back up a bit here. Take me back to the beginning. Take me through your evening. Bronwyn, you suggested trying out the urban legend about ghosts pushing cars along Sweet Hollow Road—what happened next?

BN: Aaron and I picked up Eddie and Gina. We all went to Starbucks. I told them my idea. Then we drove out to the road, around 8:30 p.m., I guess. Aaron drove us under the overpass and kept going then turned around and did it again, just goofing, pretending he couldn't stop the car there because every time he put his foot on the brake, spirits shoved on the trunk to keep us moving.

AR: Yeah. [Aaron chuckled] I said the ghosts were fed up with people making them push parked cars back and forth. They just wanted some rest. I mean, come on, if you were the ghost of some grade-schooler and people kept tricking you into pushing their car around, wouldn't you get tired of it after a while? Wouldn't you be like, piss off, and leave us alone? Plus it let me drive past the cemetery a few times to set the mood.

BK: But you did stop.

AR: Yeah. Everyone yelled at me, so I pulled onto the shoulder, killed the engine, put the car in neutral, shut the lights, and waited. Nothing happened.

EG: Another car drove by and stopped beneath the overpass.

AR: I don't remember that.

GP: I do. It was a weird car.

BN: I saw it too.

BK: Weird how, Gina?

GP: All black. Even the windows and the hubcaps. I've seen cars like that. Matte black Jeeps and Cybertrucks, custom jobs for dudes with money to burn who think they're Batman. This wasn't that, though. No make I've ever seen before. It looked like someone took a Cadillac, a Porsche, and a Honda Accord and mashed them all into one crazy Frankenstein car.

BK: How about the license plates?

GP: I didn't see them.

BK: Anyone see them?

[No one saw the plates.]

BK: How long did the black car stay parked there?

GP: It didn't park.

EG: It slowed way down. It even kind of looked like it stopped, but it didn't. It kept moving past us, super slow. That was messed up. The car wheels weren't turning, and the side of the overpass foundation was moving, not the car. Like it was gliding? Does any of this make any sense? You ever take the Long Island Rail Road and the train on the next track pulls out, and you think your train is moving, but it's standing still? Like that.

BK: Yeah, I know what you mean. What did the car do next?

BN: It went out the other side of the tunnel, and we didn't see it again. But there was something else — Aaron's dashboard clock was blinking. It had the wrong time. It said almost an hour had passed, but we'd only been sitting there for maybe twenty minutes.

EG: That's when we all lost our cell signals. I mean, yeah, there are dead zones all over Long Island, but we'd had full bars — then we didn't. Like the whole system crashed. And we have three different providers among us.

BK: What happened next?

BN: Aaron looked at the rearview mirror, then he looked over his shoulder out the back window. I was next to him when he started waving his arms at something flying at his face. He thrashed around in his seat. He shouted. It didn't make sense. He yelled, "Get away from me," "Don't touch me," and "No" a bunch of times. The stuff Eddie said too. I tried to calm him. I grabbed his shoulder, but he slapped my hand away, and that shocked me because he never touched me like that before.

AR: Holy shit, Bron, did I really do that? I'm so sorry. I had no idea.

BN: I don't think you knew you were doing it. You didn't know it was me touching you. He bucked the seat so bad, Gina yelped when the back slammed into her knees.

EG: I tried to stop him thrashing from the back seat. That's when he ran. He opened the door, slipped out of my hands, and bolted. Cold flooded in when he opened the door. I felt like I was choking because the air got so icy. Then Bronwyn took off after him. I took off after her and dragged Gina with me. I didn't want to leave her alone, but I couldn't let Bronwyn go after Aaron by herself.

BK: That's when you all entered the woods.

EG: Right, chasing Aaron.

BK: Once you were away from the car, did you see him?

BN: We glimpsed him ahead of us, running, but the farther we went after him…

BK: Yes?

BN: The farther into the woods we went after him the darker it got. We were away from the road, and, yeah, it should've been dark, but this was different.

BK: Like the darkness around us before we found Aaron?

BN: Right.

BK: Eddie, you said in the woods you felt the ground change under your feet. What'd you mean?

EG: Just what I said, man. We were walking then everything felt different. I took my eyes off the trail for, like, a fraction of a second, and when I looked again, the trees were different sizes, they were standing in different places, and what little I could see of the actual trail went in a different direction than it had. Like a maze that changes itself randomly in a video game. Some shit like that. I was actually afraid we could get stuck in there walking forever and never find our way back to the car. That's when Bronwyn saw your light.

BK: Did you see Aaron again after that?

BN: No, we'd totally lost him, but I knew he still had to be there somewhere. Like you said. We live on Long Island. How lost can you get?

GP: I made us go back to the car. We hadn't seen Aaron. I didn't think we would find him in the dark. That stuff Eddie said? That was making me sick and dizzy. I thought I might vomit. So I said we should go back and get help.

BN: It made me dizzy too, but I figured worry was making me sick. We saw your light and walked to it. You know the rest.

AN: What the hell happened to me? You guys are saying I had some kind of… episode? Like a psychotic break? A hallucination? Are you kidding? You make it sound like someone spiked my mochaccino with LSD. You have to be kidding. Are you pranking me? Because that's not cool, not at all. And, you, Keep, I don't' even know you. How the hell are you even in on this? Why would you let them put you up to such a sick gag?

BN: It's not a gag, Aaron. It all happened how we say.

AR: Bullshit. Don't touch me!

[Aaron reacted to Bronwyn putting her arm around him. The interview paused here for Bronwyn, who broke into tears, to regain her composure and continue. Muted arguing occurred. Eddie and Gina defended Bronwyn to Aaron and pleaded with him to keep an open mind. Aaron refused to believe he acted how they described but admitted to large gaps in his memory of the night and for the time spent in the woods.]

AR: Bron, I'm sorry, this is just too fucking much to believe. I mean, how can I have done what you say and not remember it or have any idea why I did it? They checked me out from head to toe in the hospital last night, right? No drugs in my system, no signs of a seizure or any kind of mental crack-up, right? Clean bill of health. How can this be?

BK: What you experienced last night, Aaron, was due to contact with phenomena beyond reality, beyond the every day. There are so many stories about that part of Long Island for a reason. It's a place where different levels of reality overlap in a way that lets them bleed through to each other. A nexus. You all experienced classic signs of an encounter. The black car. Interference with your electronics and your car's engine. Lost time. Sensory experiences that make no sense. What you experienced doesn't mean you're unhealthy or damaged. You were in the right place at the right time for forces from outside our reality to touch you.

AR: [long, loud laughter] You have got to be shitting me. Okay, smart guy, so what happened to me in the woods? How did *you* find me when my friends couldn't? Was I doing shots with little green men or those bug-eyed gray guys when you caught up to me? Let's hear it. What do you say happened?

[Benjamin recounted the search for Aaron with Annetta and Bronwyn, both of whom elaborate on the report with their own impressions. Both confirmed the same sensory deprivation and disorientation as Benjamin after the creature turned the light of its red eyes on them. Aaron remained silent through the entire account. Hearing this part of the story for the first time, Eddie and Gina gave occasional replies of shock or disgust at the state in which they found Aaron. At the end of the telling, Bronwyn broke down into sobs again. A long silence filled the recording before Aaron finally responded.]

AR: No. No fucking way. You're a fake and a liar. You're a lunatic. I am outta here. If any of you people who're supposed to be my fucking friends believe this asshole, don't bother coming with me, don't bother calling me because we are fucking done.

CHAPTER SEVEN

Annetta and I took a break from the investigation and spent a few days celebrating Christmas. We decorated a small tree with old ornaments from my parents' stash in the basement, played Christmas carols on the Bluetooth speaker, and baked sugar cookies. We even drank egg nog and wrapped a few presents for each other. I gave Annetta a cashmere sweater and leather boots. She gave me a new telephoto lens for my digital SLR and a Loch Ness Monster T-shirt, ordered from Scotland. We watched a few Christmas movies, expecting an intruding knock at the door or a black car pulling into the driveway at any moment. Neither came, nor did any other disturbance break our peace, as if the sub-rosa powers-that-be had given us a few days off.

By silent agreement, we avoided discussing what we'd witnessed in the woods. We both thought about it, almost non-stop, and from time to time one or the other of us would take a seat at the dining room table where we'd spread out our notes, maps, interview transcripts, and other research, and noodle through it. As much as we enjoyed the quiet time, we couldn't resist the urge to scratch that itch, to see if some notion or connection that floated up from the depths of our brains made sense of things. None did, though, and neither of us really expected them to—not at that point. Despite the intensity of our encounters and those reported to us, whatever intended to reveal itself to us seemed stuck in the early, confusing, scattershot stages of its unveiling—assuming it even intended to reveal anything at all.

The possibility existed that it meant only to contact Karina Clemente, the Palmieri ladies, and Aaron Reynolds, and not us, that we'd seen what we had only because we knew how to see beyond its camouflage, the way optical illusions lose their potency once your eyes decipher the trick. I didn't believe that nor did Annetta, but we couldn't rule it out.

The day after Christmas proved unseasonably warm, high 40s to low 50s, and sunny. I convinced Annetta to return to the West Hills to hike the ground by daylight. We reached the trail head a little before noon and hiked east toward Sweet Hollow Road, approaching the area where we'd found Aaron. An hour later, taking our time, hoping to recognize some scar in a tree trunk or an array of bare branches to confirm we were in the right place, we felt defeated. Earth thudded solid underfoot. Leaves crunched. The landscape played tricks on us. No fog or haze cottoned the air. Visibility remained clear and sharp. After a time, we emerged at Sweet Hollow Road about twenty yards from the Northern State overpass. Tracks in the mud showed where we'd parked our car. A discarded Starbuck's cup from Aaron's car lay crushed at the base of the overpass support wall.

I shot photos of it all, documented our hike, the tracks, and debris. I switched to the new lens Annetta had gifted me then backed down the road and snapped shots of the overpass from a distance. We walked back into the woods, struggling to retrace our steps from the night of the 22nd, but the darkness had been so thick and synthetic I doubted we'd seen the real landscape even as we walked over it.

"You get the feeling, maybe, we're looking for a place that doesn't exist?" I said.

"It was so damn dark that night, I think we could be standing in the exact right spot and never know it," Annetta said.

"It feels different here today. Less electric. Less dense. And listen," I said, as I tilted my camera to photograph a bird in a tall, barren oak tree. It flapped away as the shutter clicked when two squirrels emerged from a leafy nest and chased each other along veiny branches. "Hear the animals? It's all normal. I didn't hear a thing in the woods that night but us stamping around and yelling. Either the animals were all hiding or they were locked out of wherever we found Aaron."

"Locked out," Annetta said, no question, mulling over the idea.

We continued along the meandering trails, soaking in the atmosphere. Wind rose, chasing away the morning stillness. At a trail intersection, I aimed my camera west and scanned the trees. Light flashed as I moved my lens. I jerked it back to focus on the flicker of a piece of reflective metal or glass. At first, I couldn't find it, but when it sparkled again, I zoomed in on it—until it blinked three times, each one successively brighter. The final glare hurt my eyes. I grunted and lowered the camera.

"You all right?" Annetta said.

Rubbing my eyes, I said, "Fine, just a glare intensified by the lens. Probably a sun catcher or crystal wind chimes in someone's yard reflecting the sun."

"Lemme see." I handed the camera to Annetta and pointed. "I got it. Yeah, something shiny. It's twitching… no, spinning. A silver spiral. A garden fascinator, maybe, or—ouch!"

Annetta lowered the camera, shut her eyes, and shook her head.

"Got you too, huh?"

"Hmm, like getting snow-blinded. I can still see the shape." Bringing the camera back to her eye, she zoomed in and surveyed the yard around the flashing item. "Hey, you know what? That's the Palmieri house."

"What? Seriously?"

"Oh, yeah. Whatever is flashing us is in their backyard. You know what else?" Handing my camera back to me, she marked the position of the sun overhead then turned east. "It's in a straight line from where we pulled off on Sweet Hollow Road."

Comparing the sun's current location to where it hung in the sky when we started, I eyed trees through the camera until I zoomed in on the Northern State overpass through the mesh of branches. I offered Annetta the camera. "Look there. It's the overpass too."

Annetta declined the camera. "I believe you. What does it mean?"

"Hell if I know," I said. "It's just a weird coincidence, isn't it?"

Annetta laughed. "Unrelated events in which the universe sometimes echoes itself and lends significance to trivial details."

"This feels different. Like there's intention behind it."

"Maybe, but how does that even help? We've got one Mothman sighting miles from here on the Ocean Parkway—then another with the Mothman acting like a b-movie monster. In any of the original reports or sightings, was the Mothman ever violent? I never heard about him sucking out people's brains."

The question had nagged both of us for the past several days. We knew what we'd seen, what it looked like, what our brains wanted to identify it as—yet the pieces fit only superficially.

"No, the general consensus on the Mothman—excluding those who chalk it off to badly lit sightings of great horned owls and sandhill cranes—is that he came to warn people about the Silver Bridge disaster. Like an omen. A banshee. A cryptid prophet trying to divert people from an ill-fated road. A helper seeking to save lives. There are some really far out theories that the Mothman was a guardian angel."

"Guardian angels don't stick insect feelers into people's heads," Annetta said.

"Not as far as we know, but… would it be any weirder than half the other stuff we've encountered if they did?" I said.

Annetta laughed. My phone buzzed in my pocket. I fished it out and eyed the screen. I blinked twice before I brought myself to thumb the green circle to answer it. The caller ID read: ETHAN SCAPETTI. No profile picture. Would I have even recognized Ethan, though? He had disappeared a few years ago, along with his girlfriend, Lana, and no one I knew had seen him since then. I had never erased his number from my phone.

"Hello?" I said. "Ethan? Is this you, amigo?"

Static filled my ear. Then as if the electronic clicks and hums coalesced into coherency, a voice, most definitely Ethan's, said, "Hey, yeah, buddy, it's me. Long time no chat, I know, but it's hard to make a call from where me and Lana wound up."

"Where are you? Where have you been? Are you okay?" I asked, the first of a whirlwind list of questions gushing through my mind to reach my lips.

"Listen, man, I have to warn you. You and Annetta broke some rules. You crossed some lines. Saw things you shouldn't have. Caught attention you don't want. You keep digging up this Mothman stuff? You might vanish like me and Lana, that is, if you don't wind up dead first. Take my advice. Leave it be. Check the group—Lana's group—if you don't believe me. Gotta go now. Miss you, brother."

Ethan's voice faded into clicks and crackles then died.

The call ended.

The phone dropped from my trembling hand.

CHAPTER EIGHT

It took Annetta almost fifteen minutes to calm me enough to hike out of the preserve. She drove us home. Hours later, the echo of Ethan's voice in my head still made me shiver. Ethan had introduced me to the world of the bizarre, the mysterious, and the paranormal, had inadvertently led to my marriage to Annetta, and changed the entire course of my life. All by chance, I had once thought—but not since my understanding of the high strangeness that seemed to govern my life had deepened. A black car, the kind I'd come to know too well, had caused the accident that laid up Ethan, so I wound up with his assignment to interview Patricia Sung, a lady who claimed to have the remains of the Montauk Monster, with Annetta as my expert. Not long after that, Ethan and his girlfriend Lana disappeared. The last I saw or heard of them were photos of unknown origin showing the two descending into the abandoned, underground military base at Camp Hero in Montauk, and a reassuring letter from Ethan I doubted he'd actually written. After all we went through at the time, all the weirdness, all the unsettling intrusions into our lives, I thought I'd never hear from or see Ethan again, which raised an obvious question that Annetta, thankfully, waited to ask until we reached home and had warm coffee at hand.

"Was it really Ethan? How could you tell if it wasn't?" she asked. "Worse, how could know for sure if it was?"

"It was him," I told her, "I can't explain how I know that. I just do. It sounded like him, felt like him, reminded me perfectly of him. I haven't heard his voice in a few years now, and my brain didn't hesitate to identify it. Do you understand? Some people you know, you don't interact with them for a while, you need a few seconds to match their face or voice with a name or your memories of them. Not this time. It was Ethan. I won't be upset if you doubt it. Hell, it's a good idea if you do just to keep us balanced. But I know."

"Okay, let's say it was Ethan. Why did he call? Where the hell are he and Lana? Why didn't he ever contact you before today?"

I shrugged. "I told you everything he said. I think our location helped him make contact. That place, those woods, that land is a swamp of weirdness. Something is stirring it up. I guess he found a channel to get through."

Annetta swallowed, nodded, then placed a hand on my knee. "You understand what you're saying, right?"

"What do you mean?"

"You're talking as if he and Lana are not part of our world anymore."

"Dammit, Annetta, they haven't been part of our world for a long time. They walked off into some hole in reality, and—" I snapped my fingers "—ceased to be! How many times could the same thing have happened to us? We entered the same tunnels they did beneath Camp Hero, but we came out. What if we never did? What if winding up in that freakish billabong, chasing the Bunyip, had been a one-way trip? We would've been erased from the earth like them. The only difference is we have no one like us to even guess at where we'd gone."

I snapped my mouth shut and grimaced as I heard my tone of voice. The tension at the corner of Annetta's eyes receded. I had stopped short of upsetting her, regained my composure, and yanked myself back from the brink of foolishness. She didn't deserve my anger or panic. Not after everything we'd confronted together and all the times we'd pulled each other back from a ledge of madness. But a terrifying thought came on the heels of my truncated rant, one I suspect had lurked in my subconscious for a long time, weighted to its depths by the sheer horror of it.

"What if," I said, pausing to calm my breathing, "each time we entered those places we came out not in our original world but one just slightly removed from it. One almost exactly the same but some cosmic micro-distance closer to all the raw chaos and weirdness we've glimpsed along the way? What if we did disappear like Ethan and Lana and never even noticed."

Annetta set her mug on the coffee table and stood. She paced the living room, her brow furrowed, her lips moving almost unnoticeably as she worked through her train of thought. I sat back on the sofa and sipped my coffee, now tepid and bitter, the caffeine doing nothing to help my frayed nerves. I placed my mug next to hers then pressed the heels of my hands to my eyes and tried to rub away a growing headache.

"Okay, okay." Annetta ceased pacing. "I hear you. But now it's my turn to ask you to go with me on this. We are where we started, where we belong, the one real world. Or at least our real world. Okay?"

"Why are you so sure? Doesn't it add up that the more we've interacted with the weird stuff, the more of it we've encountered because we've drifted closer to the source?"

"It makes a kind of sense, yeah, but it's not what happened. I just know it's not. Okay? Like you knew with Ethan, I know this. I'd feel it in my bones, in my soul, if we'd... what do we even call this? Traveled? Jumped? Fell? It doesn't matter. If we weren't living in our one and only reality, I'd feel it."

I shook my head. "I trust you. I want to believe that, but... why?"

Annetta sat down and grabbed my hand. "Because the weird stuff doesn't seem any less weird. Because 'strange' only means something when 'normal' exists. Because all the intrusions into reality we've experienced suggest this place matters somehow to the entire workings of the universe. That it's unique. Otherwise, why keep targeting us for this stuff? The Men in Black, the Bigfoot, the Men Who Are Not There, hell, even Patty Sung, her couch potato hubby, and their barn full of taxidermy oddities—all of them interacted with us because... they need an anchor in reality. Our reality."

Annetta's words sank in and chased my wild idea and the fear associated with it back to the sub-chambers of my mind. Not as deep as before but enough that my rising panic subsided.

"The only question is what do we do with that? Or about it?" she said. "We've figured it out in the past, but this time feels different. And, damn it, is this stuff going to fill the rest of our lives? What the hell do they want us to do this time?"

"How about we start where Ethan pointed us?"

"Where's that?"

"Lana's online group," I said. "That has to be what he meant by check the group, the online, paranormal discussion group she ran. I assumed it was dead without her to moderate it. I checked it now and then for a few months after they vanished. I hoped one of them might turn up there. It was full of people asking about her, but the chatter died down. Losing Lana seemed to rob it of its purpose, so I stopped looking."

I retrieved my laptop from the dining room, returned to the sofa, and booted it up. I still had the group bookmarked, and it flickered to life on my screen in a few seconds. Lana's group dated back to her teens and used an outdated board platform, but its members liked it that way. A touch out of step with the moment made it a little harder to find. It kept away people less serious than them about the topics they discussed—or at least they believed so, and maybe it did. None of that mattered much now. A quick skim of topics and threads showed no new posts for more than a year, no new threads for almost eighteen months, a functionally dead space, a digital ghost town whose residents had migrated to the greener pastures of newer, flashier social media— except for a single thread from eight weeks ago, its title in all caps, pinned to the top: LOOKING FOR BENJAMIN KEEP. Started by ultraterrestrial121567, the post count showed 46 comments. All of them, I discovered after opening it, came from the same user.

All of them asked for help contacting me.

CHAPTER NINE

"How do we know she's really who she says she is?" Annetta said.

"We don't yet," I said. "But why would she lie, especially about stuff we were able to verify already?"

"It's weird how she made contact. You and me, sweetie? We aren't all that hard to find."

"Not since we stopped trying to hide, no. But people cling to the familiar when they're spooked, and Lana is a connection to us."

My eyes itched from the hot air blasting from the dashboard vents. I lowered the heat and fan then sighed. We had arrived an hour early for our meeting and parked on the far side of the lot from the entrance to The Library of Alexandra, "Home to Forgotten, Lost, and Special Books," as the sign above the door touted. Annetta and I knew the shop—and the owner, Alexandra—well. It provided a comfortable, public place to meet people who made us think twice about their intentions and motives.

A white, late model BMW, as clean as if it had come straight from a car wash, rolled in and took a space near the door. The driver, a woman, emerged, dragging a swollen canvas tote bag, which she slung over her shoulder. She locked her car then pulled her overcoat closed as she scurried into the shop. She glanced at the front table displays, checked her watch, then settled at an unoccupied table in the café area.

"Ready?" I said.

"Let's go make a new friend," Annetta said.

The woman behind the counter, Marianna, a twenty-something with purple streaks in her hair and an impressive array of piercings, nodded as we entered. We returned the greeting as we walked to the café. Three patrons browsed the stacks: a mother and daughter in the children's book section and an elderly man with a cane and a crewcut who browsed the history aisle. Our new friend stared at her phone screen so intently, she didn't notice us until I cleared my throat. She had draped her overcoat on her seatback and wore a snug, black sweater, gold hoop earrings, and her chestnut hair in a longish bob. She looked only a few years older than me but haggard beyond her age. It showed mainly in her knobby, wrinkled fingers and the creases at the corners of her eyes.

"Mrs. Cowan?" I said. "I'm Ben Keep. This is Annetta Maikels."

She jolted and placed her phone face down on the table, then stood and extended her hand. "Ramona, please. Thank you for meeting with me. Can I treat you to some coffee?"

"Sure," Annetta said, as we took two of the four seats at the table.

I waved for Marianna, who came and took our coffee orders.

"What a lovely shop," Ramona said. "I never knew it was here."

"It's a booklover's gold mine," I said. "Especially if you're looking for stuff out of print or out of the mainstream."

"Is that why you come here? Seeking esoteric texts for your research?"

Ramona laughed, struggling to make herself comfortable, so I chuckled at her joke.

"Sometimes. Other times, just looking for a good beach read. And I like the coffee."

"Of course," she said. "I loved to read as a kid, all the way through college, but then you get into the real world, and who the hell has time to read for pleasure anymore? I mean, life's just a jumbled ball of chaos these days, don't you think? All these social media notifications flying at you, pings from all the apps for bills and your bank accounts, and the weather updates, and, oh, the ads! They're inescapable. Such a deluge, I can barely even figure out what they're selling me half the time. It's all too much, isn't it? On top of a career and keeping house and keeping up with family, and… it's been a long time since my cousin, Lana, vanished. I miss her dearly. I'd give almost anything to have her back, even to just know where she went, if she's still alive. You don't… you don't know anything about what happened to her, do you?"

Marianna served our coffees, adding a plate of thumbprint cookies she knew Annetta liked.

"If you're hoping for news about Lana, we have none to offer," I said. "One of my best friends disappeared with her, and I've got no idea how or where to."

"Oh, I know that. Ethan Scapetti, yes. It's not that. It's that I've been, um, seeing things?" Ramona lifted her coffee mug with a trembling hand, pressed it to her lips, and slurped. "Things I can't explain. So, maybe you could help me with that. It's the kind of thing I'd have asked Lana about when we were kids. She could explain that stuff in a way that made me feel better. At ease with it. We were as close as sisters. All the times we stayed up talking about the weird, wild stuff she loved. Was the Loch Ness monster real? Had I ever seen a ghost? Where did Bigfoot go that made him so hard to find? That stuff didn't really interest me, but Lana dragged me into it, and I learned a lot from her. Me, though, I always wanted normal stuff. If I started the conversation it was about dolls, or baking with our moms, or the books I was reading, or my favorite cartoons. I didn't want to think about that weird stuff so much because I really wanted to get away from it—but it wouldn't let me."

"What do you mean?" asked Annetta.

"Like I said, I see things." Ramona took a deep, steadying breath. "They're not really there, but I see them. All the time growing up, even when I was too young to realize they were—not hallucinations, mind you—but glimpses of things invisible to everyone else. I hardly ever talked about it because my family treated me differently when I did. Took me to see doctors who told me it was all in my head. Made me take pills. But none of it changed what I saw. Only Lana believed me. Eventually I talked about it to her, no one else. When I turned twenty-two, it stopped. I don't know how or why. Lana didn't either. She had a dozen theories but no answer. I didn't care. I was thrilled I was normal. But it hurt my relationship with Lana. I wanted to take advantage to distance myself from all that strange stuff. She wanted to experiment on me to see if she could turn my 'second sight' on again. That's what she called it. That was a big no from me, so we drifted apart because she couldn't stop pestering me about it. I couldn't risk caving into her. She could really twist my arm at times."

"Ramona, have you started seeing things again?" I said.

"Um-hum, yes," she said.

Behind us, the elderly man paid cash for two books. The register dinged. A blast of chilly air whooshed in when he opened the door to leave. I scrutinized Ramona. Her eyes darted from me to Annetta then back again then to her coffee or the front window or the register, always in motion, but avoiding looking over my left shoulder at the nearest row among the stacks.

"What things did you see before the visions stopped?" Annetta asked.

"At first, it was animals. Cats and dogs mostly. Rabbits and squirrels. Birds. They showed up in my room. I was so little I thought the drawings in my picture books had come to life. It was things like that. Lana figured out from how I described them that some were our neighbor's pets. I'd describe one, and she'd say, oh, that's the so-and-so's cat or dog, it got hit by a car last week. I started seeing people when I got older. I knew from the very first one it was a ghost because the first person I saw was my friend Jana's grandmother. She gave us cookies and milk after school some days. I knew she'd died. Then I saw her in my room. I told Lana about that one, and she made her mom get her a Quija board for her birthday. We tried séance-y stuff, but none of it worked. I saw stuff when I saw it. Ghosts were the most normal stuff I saw."

I glanced over my shoulder, down the shadowed aisle of the crime fiction and mystery shelves, all the way to the back where wine books were shelved. Empty. The mother and her daughter completed their selection and purchased two chapter books. A teenage couple entered and skimmed through the graphic novels section. A woman talking softly on a Bluetooth earbud ordered coffee and took the comfy, wingback armchair in a far corner of the shop.

"What were the weirdest things you saw?" I asked.

"Men in black suits and hats, who would sit at my desk in the middle of the night. They looked like giants sitting at a child's desk. These little men with spindly bodies and hairy faces. They had big eyes and ears. I call them the Floor People because they rise up out of the floor. And the Air Eels. They're iridescent ribbons that undulate all around us. They pass right through you, and you never know it. At the beach or a big lake, I see creatures from the size of a giant snake to larger than a blue whale swimming under the water. Sometimes pets—not regular ones. They're like alien raccoons with shimmering fur. And these funny, little spiders with four extra legs, and I could never catch one of those, but I tried because they seemed so real. Every once in a while, I see one of the Tall Boys. I don't know what they are. All I see are their legs that reach up into the sky so far everything else is out of sight. They cover a mile or more when they take a step, but they never actually get anywhere. Like they're on some kind of treadmill. Stuff like that."

"This is what you're seeing now?" Annetta said.

"Some of it. There are new ones, and they frighten me." Ramona brushed a cookie crumb from her sweater. "I know it sounds horrible, but if you grew up with it, like me, and it never hurt you, which none of the things I saw ever did, and it brought me and Lana closer for a while, then you learn to live with it like I did. It's part of your life. I didn't even mind much at first when it came back. It made me feel close to Lana again. I hoped one day I would see her, and she'd tell me what happened. Then I started seeing new things. One thing I see almost anytime, anywhere, over and over, day and night, for a few seconds or a few minutes, but every time I see it, it leaves me feeling all hollowed out, like I'd just heard about a death in the family."

"What thing?" I asked.

"I don't know. Sometimes, it's thin and gangly like a scarecrow. Others, it's muscular and has claws like movie monster. It reminds me of an alien or a giant insect, but it's none of those. The only consistent things about it are it has enormous black wings, shaped like a butterfly's wings, and glaring red eyes."

"When's the last time you saw it?" I said, hair already rising along my neck and arms.

"Well, um, I see it right now." Ramona pointed. I stared into the empty aisle of crime and mystery books, nothing between the stacks but shadows and dust motes. "It's been watching us since you got here."

Chapter Ten

Transcript of an audio recording made by Benjamin Keep interviewing Ramona Cowan, coder, cousin of Lana Swift, age 36, recounting her experiences during the second half of 20 – , culminating in a significant "vision" on December 2.

Benjamin Keep: Thanks for agreeing to record this, Ramona. It helps us to document it.

Ramona Cowan: That's fine, I understand. You and Annetta are the first people in years who didn't look at me funny when I talked about this stuff. It's a relief to open up.

BK: Great, so let's start earlier this year. We'll come back later to questions about what you experienced growing up and your relationship with Lana, but first I want to dig into the events that led you to contact me.

RC: Six months ago, I'd never heard of you. That's when my visions resumed. I hadn't had one for almost fourteen years and then — hey, Ramona, your creepy ghost friends are back! Did you miss us? The first one came at Jones Beach. Gabe — my husband — and I went for dinner at the restaurant then for a stroll along the boardwalk. We watched the sunset while we ate, and it was dark as we walked. Not the boardwalk. That's well lit. But the beach, the surf, the dunes, and the beach grass all dropped off into shadows around us. It's funny to hear the waves break without seeing them but know how close you are to the ocean. I saw it first on the beach but didn't realize it. The lights of ships were visible in the distance. Yachts, fishing charters, even cargo ships at the horizon's edge, lined up, waiting to enter port. I thought its red eyes were lights on a ship. We reached the eastern end of the boardwalk before I understood I was seeing something else. Gabe and I sat on a bench for a while, facing the blackness of the ocean, holding hands, relaxing. Gabe knows about my visions even though they stopped before I met him. I told him everything. I didn't want to deceive him about who he was marrying—and if it changed how he felt about me, better to find out before saying, 'I do.' But it didn't. He doesn't believe in those things, but he believed I believed everything I said. Even Lana liked him for that. She told me so at my wedding. In the back of my mind, always, was the fear my visions would restart—and now that they have, I haven't had the heart to tell him. I don't want to expose him to it. I feel sort of responsible for Lana's disappearance. If she hadn't had me as a cousin, maybe she wouldn't have latched on to all the weird stuff, never would've started her paranormal group, never would've fallen down whatever rabbit hole took her away from me. Do you think it's wrong of me to keep it from him?

BK: Not everyone is built to cope with the paranormal. You're protecting him. That's admirable.

RC: Thank you. I'm hoping once I do what the visions want they'll stop again, and I won't ever have to tell him. If they go on too long, though, I have to let him know. Right? It's not fair for me to choose for him. To believe or not to believe. To step into my world or stay outside, I mean.

BK: That's a tough question, Ramona. I don't have an easy answer. Let's get back to what you saw on the boardwalk. I assume Gabe didn't see it.

RC: He didn't. I did my best not to freak out on him, but he sensed I was upset. I passed it off as work stress, and he didn't push me. Really, it was the thing on the beach. Those red lights that I'd thought belonged to a ship had grown larger the farther we moved down the boardwalk. They paced us the way the moon seems to travel with you when you're moving in a straight line. The getting bigger part, I told myself, was because the boat was moving closer to shore. By the time we sat on the bench, I'd almost convinced myself. Then I saw the shape. A black silhouette, very difficult to discern, but when it moved, it blotted out the faraway ship lights and the slivers of light reflected by the breakers. I thought it was a jumbo beach umbrella rolling in the wind. But the red lights moved with it. They started out small, but as the thing trundled closer, they irised to the size of saucers. The air turned very still and quiet. No one was within fifty yards, which was strange for a busy summer night, but it was late, near closing time for the park. I don't know if Gabe sensed the change in the air or noticed the quiet. He was preoccupied with me, asking if I was okay, but the heavy air muted his voice. The black shape rushed forward and straightened to maybe ten feet tall. Its eyes widened to the size of dinner plates and red light beamed out of them directly onto me. Everything turned sheer black and red, like looking through a ruby quartz lens. My face tingled. A buzzing sensation spread through my whole body—then it stopped. The red light, the black shape, vanished. I faced Gabe, who had a hand on my shoulder and was asking me if I was okay. I told him I was, though, of course, I wasn't, and we left. Since then, I've had visions like that almost every day.

BK: I can't imagine the toll that's taken on you.

RC: Oh, no, don't worry about that. I grew up with it. I know how to cope. They just show up in the weirdest places. I'll be at work, look up, and there's one of the men in a black suit and hat at my coworker's desk while she's out to lunch. I look out the kitchen window while filling the coffee pot with water, and there's the shape with the red eyes peeking out at me from behind a tree. The Floor People like to watch me shower, the little pervs. I've seen the Tall Boys only a few times, thank god, because they frighten me the most. I can't express how much they dwarf everything around them. They make me feel like a microbe. I see all my old weirdo companions now and then, but I've seen the red-eyed thing the most often. It's stalking me—but I don't think it means me any harm. It wants something from me. I think it doesn't know how to communicate that to me. Does that make sense?

BK: Communication between us and these entities is rarely direct. They tend to nudge us into place and hope we fill in the blanks for ourselves.

RC: Exactly. That's why I chose that username for Lana's old group.

BK: ultraterrestrial121567?

RC: Lana used to talk about this idea of beings from "beyond earth," ultraterrestrials, that poked their noses into our business. She read about them.

BK: John Keel wrote about them in *The Mothman Prophecies*, his book about the Mothman encounters and the Silver Bridge disaster.

RC: Is that the thing I'm seeing? The Mothman?

BK: Maybe. Your descriptions sound similar, but these things are rarely what they seem. Is that why you picked the date at the end of your username?

RC: Date?

BK: December 15, 1967. The date of the Silver Bridge collapse. A stress crack of 0.1 inch in one of the key links of the bridge caused a failure that collapsed the entire structure into the freezing Ohio River. Forty-six people died. Some believe the Mothman appearances in the region around that time were intended as a warning of the imminent disaster because the flaw in the structure was almost undetectable.

RC: No, I didn't know any of that. Oh my god, that's awful. But I just added random numbers to make my account go through because someone else had already picked "ultraterrestrial." At least I thought they were random. Sometimes things come to me days or weeks after a vision. A detail I overlooked. A new idea. A deeper understanding of what I saw. Could that be why I picked the date? The Mothman planted them in my mind? Is that a thing it does? Is it psychic? What the hell even is it? A ghost, a monster, an ultraterrestrial entity?

BK: I wish I knew.

RC: You and me both.

RC: So this Mothman thing showed up in Ohio almost sixty years ago? Where else has it popped up since then?

BK: West Virginia, not Ohio. The sightings at that time occurred on the West Virginia side of the Ohio River on rural roads around an old TNT factory. It's not like Bigfoot or UFOs, turning up everywhere, but reports have come from a few other places. If it helps you at all, Ramona, you're not the only one who has seen him around here recently.

RC: What?

BK: Annetta and I have been collecting reports of sightings of a creature like the one you see. We even encountered it ourselves less than a week ago.

RC: Are you gaslighting me?

BK: Not at all, no. We didn't say anything earlier because we didn't want to influence what you told us, but it's clear now that something like what happened in '67 is occurring on Long Island.

RC: Tell me. Now. Everything you know. Everything you've seen. Please!

At this point, Ben and Annetta share with Ramona accounts of the Clementes's report, their own encounter with the Mothman while finding Aaron Reynolds, and the Palmieris's run-in with the Men in Black. Ben provided a rough summary of the Long Island connections to the original Mothman sightings and the strange background of Mount Misery. Ramona gasped several times but refrained from interrupting.

RC: Why here? Why now?

BK: No idea. A warning? Not about a bridge that's going to collapse. That doesn't make sense here. Another kind of disaster? Or no reason at all? Mount Misery and West Hills have a history of weird occurrences. A lot of that is urban legend, but maybe not all. Maybe reality and wherever these things come from overlaps a little too much there. That's where we were when Ethan called and told me to check Lana's group. I wouldn't have seen your posts otherwise.

RC: Holy shit! You talked to Ethan?

A fresh round of conversation ensued as Ben explained his contact with Ethan and apologized for having learned nothing to shed light on Lana's whereabouts. The recording paused here when Ramona asked for a break and a glass of water. When the interview resumed, Ramona's voice sounded deep and raspy as if she might have been crying or was holding back anger.

RC: This happened in late October while Gabe and I were coming home late from a party at his friend's house in Bellmore. We left around midnight. It was a beautiful night, and we had to go right past the entrance to the Wantagh Parkway anyway, so we decided to take the scenic route. Gabe had been drinking. I was driving. By the time I got on the Ocean Parkway, Gabe had fallen asleep. I kept the radio low and savored the quiet, the lack of traffic. You get so used to the press and rush of the Island all the time, the crowds, the cars, the lines everywhere, the roads all built out and developed, the never-ending traffic lights, the feeling everywhere you go, all the time, that someone's watching you, waiting to mess with you, wishing you out of their way, and you can never take a breath and let your guard down, and—yeah, well, all that faded away. I savored it. No traffic, no noise, a clear night sky full of stars. Time to just drive without worrying about someone cutting you off or riding your tail and flashing their high beams because you're going only fifteen over the limit.

BK: This was the same road where the Clementes had their encounter.

RC: Stop. Please don't interrupt me, or I won't be able to finish. What happened to us was not like what the Clementes saw. There was nothing on the Pencil, nothing flying around chasing my car. Near Gilgo Beach I saw a Tall Boy in the Great South Bay, but I often see them at the beach. Its mossy legs were dim. They flickered in and out the way a porch light flickers when the wind blows leaves or branches across it — then it vanished. I saw ghosts. They lined the road. Sad and lost, standing on the shoulder, watching us pass with hollow eyes. Low sounds mutter in the back of my head when I see them. Their voices, I guess. Asking for what? I don't know. They sound pleading. I think there are — or were — a lot more corpses down there than have been reported as victims of the Long Island Serial Killer. I saw enough of that stuff as a kid to thicken my skin to it. I see it, others don't. It's like I see color, and everyone else is colorblind. I'm different. Fine. It doesn't change anything. I saw nothing out of the ordinary for me along the Ocean Parkway that night. I took the same exit as the Clementes on to the Robert Moses Causeway and drove north, right over the Great South Bay Bridge without the faintest idea of the link between bridges and the Mothman. Just another drive. Late at night, yes, and a little out of our way, okay, but we were half an hour from home when the vision really started. I was driving north on the Sagtikos. Gabe was snoring in the passenger's seat. First, the sky filled with red light. We'd gone far enough that the Sagtikos had become the Sunken Meadow Parkway. After the exit for Indian Head Road, the traffic thins to nothing, especially that late. Flashing lights appeared ahead of us. An emergency vehicle, but I've never seen another one like it. The red, white, and blue lights looked like any other police or fire truck lights, but the vehicle itself — picture an ambulance combined with a fire truck then stretched out like a drag racer, but with eight rear wheels, double sets of four on either side. A crane protruded from it, and a cable threaded from the top of it stretched into the trees off the shoulder, winching a black car from a ditch. That's another thing too — I've never seen a car like it. Two men in black suits sat in the open trunk. Their legs hung over the rear bumper as the winch tugged the car from the brush. Red light glowed behind them, rising from the trunk. One of the men tipped his fedora at me, and as the driver's side window of the rescue truck came into view, a gray face like a balloon peeked out at me—then we passed and the whole scene blinked out of sight. I should've woken Gabe and asked him if he saw it too, but it happened so fast. The next exit should've been for Pulaski Road, but when the exit sign came up it was for Indian Head Road again. I made a mistake, I told myself. Misread the last sign. Became confused. Right? But then we reached the same stretch of road. No emergency vehicle, no black car, no flashing lights. No odd men. This time, the lights were deep red and steady, blaring out from the trees like laser spotlights. A thing high in the branches projected them into the night. They looked bright enough to reach the moon. I looked for where they came from, but all I saw were fluttering shadows that blended with the bare branches. This time, I nudged Gabe. He woke and looked where I pointed. The second he turned his head, the damn lights blinked out, leaving nothing for him to see. I let him drift back to sleep. Then the next exit sign came. Goddam Indian Head Road, *again*. I knew I wasn't so tired or confused that I'd gotten lost. Was I stuck in a vision? Was I really driving that same length of parkway? Or was I driving elsewhere, oblivious to the real road? Should I stop in case I hit something I couldn't see? What if stopping left me and Gabe trapped in my vision? I didn't know what to do. When I rolled up to that same patch of road, I slowed down, waiting for something to show. Nothing did at first, but then red light poured through the windshield and filled the car. I couldn't see Gabe, the road, or the sky, the trees, anything, except the silhouette of a thing resolving into solidity right in front of us. Its double-lobed wings stretched to either side, rising like a giant hand closing on us. I slammed the brakes. The tires squealed. The car skidded. I saw no way to avoid hitting the thing's thick black body—but when I expected to collide with it, the red light blinked out. The road cleared. We skidded to a stop halfway into the left lane. I caught my breath and thought about waking Gabe. But if he saw what I saw then it was real, right? Not a vision. If these incredible things could be real, what would that mean? I let him doze, hit the gas, and sped for the next exit, and, damn it, you guessed it, back to Indian Head Road. Now I screamed. Gabe shifted and muttered something but stayed asleep. I wanted to floor it past that same spot where I kept seeing things, but I was afraid of what maybe I couldn't see, so I kept my cool, my eyes on the road, and drove like nothing weird had happened. This time, I rolled right by without disruption. I spotted the tree where the lights had burned into the sky in the rearview mirror and sighed with relief. I looked at Gabe—but he was *gone*. In the passenger seat sat the Mothman, his furred black body like mossy twigs twined together, like a child's pipe cleaner doll with a bulbous head, dominated by red eyes that seemed as big as stop signs up so close. They seethed with light. Feelers sprouted from the top of its head and its mouth. They wriggled like seaweed in a slow current. I found myself breathless. My blood literally ran cold. Every part of me but my hands shivered. They locked so tight to the steering wheel my wrists ached. The thing stared right at me, into me, into my brain, my mind, my soul. Then it spoke. Or maybe I heard the words inside my head. It said: "The wheel is broken. The earth is broken. The sky is broken. Who can fix these things? These wrecks at the side of the road. These splinters in the mind's eye. Doors fallen off their hinges. All is broken and what wills it so may come and go. None is broken or all is broken." The passenger window rolled down. The thing—Mothman—folded its wings tight around it into a hunched shape, leaving only its eyes defined, then it shot out of the car. Its wings opened and blotted out the stars as it flew up and out of sight. Too stunned to let go my grip on the steering wheel, I kept driving. The next exit sign came, finally, for Pulaski Road, and Gabe reappeared snoring in the passenger seat. I cried with relief seeing him there. I pulled off the parkway and took a backway home. That's when I decided I needed help. I figured out Lana's password for her online group, signed in as an admin, and hoped someone who might know what the hell is happening to me might see it.

A long silence followed as Ben waited to make sure Ramona had finished her story.

BK: That's incredible, Ramona. I can't imagine what you felt during that encounter. I've never heard of anything like it. Thank you for sharing it.

RC: Can you help me? I still see the Mothman. Every day, sooner or later, somewhere, it comes creeping up from behind a building, or a car, or a tree, or it pops up behind me in the ladies room mirror, or it stands in front of me and vanishes as soon as I reach out. This isn't like my visions used to be. This feels… I don't know, sick? Ill. Unhealthy. Rotten. My other visions have a sense of rightness to them, as if no matter how bizarre they are, they belong in this world, are part of it, or at least part of mine. These, though, are like cancer metastasizing outside an organ, seeping where it doesn't belong, poisoning the body. They're like pressure on the brain from a cosmic head injury, and the swelling is pushing into my consciousness—and the strangest part of it? I think it wants us to know. It wants us to push back, to protect ourselves and reality, to drive out the rot and cure the sickness. My god, listen to me. I sound like a lunatic. But it's all real, I swear it is. Lana would know it, would trust me, would tell me what to do. What do I do, Ben? Please, what? Tell me.

BK: Ramona, I'm sorry. I don't know the answer. I hardly even know the right questions to ask.

RC: Someone better figure it out soon or all of this—whatever it is—swelling up around us will burst like an unchecked tumor. God help us when that happens.

CHAPTER ELEVEN

I couldn't fathom the toll Ramona's life experiences had taken on her. On one hand, she seemed more resilient and adaptable than most people who encountered paranormal phenomena. On the other, she seemed like a woman barely clinging to her sanity. Annetta and I wanted to help, but we didn't know where to start. How much of her account could we credit as potentially true, how much mere vision, how much sub-conscious elaboration and exaggeration? The thought of trying to verify her visions, their variety and consistency, daunted us, and more plausible explanations lay within easier reach. Ramona's head brimmed with the things that obsessed her lost, beloved cousin, Lana, and ordinary, but unfortunate, means, such as delusion or schizophrenia, could've brought them to life for her. The mind fills in the blanks. Present it random lights and shadows, and it makes a shape. Pareidolia. The brain organizes unrelated patterns into familiar objects such as faces, things out of myth and urban legend, out of foggy memory, or out of imagination. Only the blatant similarity of Ramona's reports to our own stopped us from dismissing them—but we still didn't know what to do about them anymore than we did those of the Clementes, the Palmieris, or Bronwyn Norris and her friends. We had reached a dead end.

By the first week of January, Annetta and I began to wonder if the wave of weirdness had passed by and moved on. Life settled back to normal. Annetta, still on break between semesters, worked on a research paper she'd been writing. I took some one-day gigs photographing fashion boutiques—really, high-end thrift shops—for a local lifestyle website producing a feature on the best places to find vintage clothes. In my downtime, I reread *The Mothman Prophecies*. I studied the past ten years of Men in Black reports. There were surprisingly few, part of a distinct trend in the overall decline of such reports from a peak in the 1960s and early '70s. I dug through our old casefiles, especially those from our Montauk Monster investigation when we first encountered the twelve-legged spiders that Ramona had also seen. From experience, I knew they could appear as small as a common wolf spider or, in their native habitat, which I'd once glimpsed, as large as a second-string, Godzilla-movie monster. When we grew tired of working, Annetta and I cozied up on the sofa and watched old comedies or played Scrabble.

A few times we went out for a drive. Twice we killed a couple of hours cruising the Ocean Parkway but found nothing but night, empty winter beaches, and ordinary traffic. One night, following a hunch, we staked out the Palmieri house, waiting for the Men in Black to show up. They never did. And one sunny Saturday morning, when the temperature hit the low 40s, I hiked every mapped trail of the Western Hills Preserve, while Annetta stayed home on a department conference call. I found no Mothman, no flashing lights, no strange darknesses, no calls from lost friends, only other hikers, people walking their dogs, all of them sublimely and frustratingly normal, real, and human. I picked up lunch from Annetta's favorite pizzeria on the way home to surprise her then spent the rest of the day brooding. Visions of twelve-legged spiders and red-eyed moths danced through my head and a forlorn notion emerged from the chaos of ideas jockeying for my conscious attention.

"They say you're never more than three feet from a spider," I said as I cleaned the remnants of two eggplant parmigiana heroes off the kitchen table.

Annetta frowned. "Not literally. That just means spiders make themselves at home everywhere."

I refilled our glasses of iced tea then sat across from Annetta. "Yeah, but spiders, they're great hiders. Right? There's probably a dozen spiders, maybe more, in this house right now, but we never see them. It's in the spring when their eggs hatch and the young go seeking places to set up their own webs or in the early winter when food is scarce that you notice them, when they move around."

"Sure, I guess," Annetta said, "but what does that say about all those months we don't see them? That there are a lot of other bugs in the house to keep them well fed?"

"Yeah, I suppose it does. Insects are always around, everywhere. Maybe that's why we see these things the way we do. Twelve-legged spiders and Mothman."

"We see a lot of things that don't look like bugs too," Annetta said.

"Right, but, I've been thinking. I had this total dump apartment in Baldwin right out of college," I said. "One night I got so creeped out there I had to go crash on a friend's couch until I could get an exterminator into my place."

"Roaches?"

"No, surprisingly, the place did not have a roach problem. It had spiders."

"How many legs did they have?"

"Eight. These were normal spiders. This was before… well, before you and I knew what to look for between the cracks in reality," I said. "I was lying on my bed, on the phone with a friend, chatting about who the hell knows what now, and staring at the ceiling fixture, a standard two-socket fixture with a frosted glass shade. I noticed the white ceiling looked spotted with gray specs. First, I thought it was mold, but then the specks moved. The pattern changed. The dots radiated from the light, spreading across the ceiling. I stood up on the bed for a closer look. Baby spiders. Hundreds of them. Maybe thousands. I mean, in the moment, it seemed like millions, a gusher of tiny, semi-translucent spider babies carpeting my bedroom ceiling. I tried to imagine that many eyes watching me while I slept, and it nauseated me. I grabbed some paper towels and started smashing. I wiped those little fuckers away, but I missed some, and they kept coming out from the light. Momma arachnid probably put her eggs there for the warmth from the bulbs. The ones I missed, I had no idea where they went. They just vanished into my bedroom. That's when I stuffed some clothes and my toothbrush into an overnight bag and hit up my friend. I had an exterminator come the next day. He couldn't find a single spider in the entire place. He sprayed and put some glue-box traps down, said call him if it happened again, but it never did. I tried not to think about it when I went to bed that night. Took me a week to sleep right again."

"Gross. Where did they go?" Annetta said.

"No idea. I lived there another eight months and never saw another spider the whole time, and, believe me, I was looking. Never found any in the glue traps, either. So did they all ditch my place for greener pastures? Did the exterminator kill them all? Did bigger spiders eat them? Who the hell knows? That's exactly my point, though. I saw them, they were there, an intrusion into my life—then they weren't. What if that's what happened here, and we've seen all we're going to see of the Mothman and the Men in Black this time around? What if it's all over with no rhyme or reason? Like an eruption into our reality that has run out of pressure. The flow has ceased."

"It's never happened like that before. The weird shit sticks until we see it through," Annetta said.

"First time for everything," I said.

"What do you think the twelve-legged spiders even are?" Annetta said.

"I think they're a lot like regular spiders and hold a unique place in the ecosystem. Most of them are harmless, even helpful. The biggest one we ever saw stopped that monster in the Green from coming into our world. Some of them can be dangerous. A few orb spiders around your house, a few wolf spiders in your basement, they cut down on mosquitos and flies that bother you. A nest of brown recluses in your attic, well, that's a tragedy waiting to happen."

"How does this help us, Ben? I mean, I hear where you're coming from, but what do we do about it?" Annetta said. "Everything we've experienced in the past weeks says something, somewhere, in the workings of reality, is broken. Do we not have to find it and fix it?"

"Maybe, but how? We don't even know where to look."

Except, as it turned out, we did know where to look, but we didn't yet know we knew it. We only figured that out after Ramona called us in a panic a week later and pleaded with us to meet her again. She had seen another vision of the Mothman, not her usual daily sightings, but a full-on experience like the night on the parkway she'd recounted to us. And it left her shaken to her core.

Chapter Twelve

We met Ramona in a café in the lobby of the building where she worked. Constructed and opened about two years ago, the building towered over its neighbors. An eighteen-floor complex that stood like a skyscraper over its surroundings, it had generated tension and controversy for years before construction commenced. People complained it would alter the character of the area and turn the suburbs into the city. Ultimately, the necessary variances to the building code were granted, the permits issued, and by the time anyone went to jail for the rampant bribes that made it all happen, the building stood tall and full of activity. Ramona waved at us through the glass wall of the café. We joined her in a booth.

"I ordered you coffee," she said. "I hope that's good. It's the least I can do after losing my shit on you over the phone. I'm sorry about that. I didn't mean to dump it on you, but I got kind of overwhelmed. I didn't know who to tell. I couldn't say anything to Gabe, especially not what I saw this time, no, that would be bad. I think he might have me committed if I did that, and then I was scrolling, looking for people online who might've had similar experiences, but I didn't find any, nothing even close, and the stuff I found sounded crazy even to me, so I didn't know where else to turn, and… I'm sorry but thank you for coming."

"How much coffee have you had?" I said.

"This is my third cup. I had two before I left the house this morning. I've been thinking about cutting back. You think I should?" she said.

Annetta placed her hand on Ramona's wrist. "Honey, take a deep breath, calm down. We're here. We want to help you. Tell us what you saw, okay?"

Ramona did as Annetta suggested then released a long exhalation. "The Mothman came into my bedroom. It filled the whole room with red light from its eyes, and it woke me up. It was perched on my headboard, and from its mouth… its tongue, whatever you call that part on a bug, snaked out and latched onto the back of Gabe's head. Then Gabe sat up and opened his eyes, but I don't think he saw me, saw anything, really, because he stared into the dark and said, 'Broken thirteen. Broken wheel. Broken wall. Broken windows. Thirteen broken wheels crash the doors. All is broken. None must be broken.' The red light brightened. I couldn't see anything else. When it faded away, Gabe lay sleeping beside me. Mothman was gone, and I couldn't stop shaking. It's trying to tell me something, trying to tell us all something, isn't it? But what? What's broken?"

"That must have been terrifying, Ramona," I said. "I wish I had answers for you. Annetta and I have been wracking our brains for weeks trying to piece all this into some kind of sense, but it's like a puzzle without all the pieces. The picture is fragmented."

"Do you remember anything else it said?" Annetta asked. "Have you had other visions so strong since we interviewed you?"

Ramona shook her head. "Just the normal stuff until that night."

I glanced into the lobby and saw a familiar face: Hector Clemente. He chatted with a man in a suit by the reception desk. A name tag pinned to his shirt displayed the logo of the property company that owned the building. A moment later, an elevator opened, and two more familiar faces appeared: Hayley Palmieri and Aaron Reynolds. I gripped Annetta's shoulder and pointed. She gasped when she recognized them all.

Life often echoes itself. The universe resonates and ripples, creates coincidences with the illusion of meaning. Synchronicities hint at a design beyond our perception fueling the engines of reality—a design that may exist only in our perceptions. Clouds float across the sky, and our minds form shapes out of random water vapor driven by the wind. Sometimes, though, on rare occasions, those signs actually mean something if you know how to read them. Neither Annetta nor I had read them right. Now the connection presented itself to us, unmistakable if unclear, a common thread we'd completely overlooked, one I couldn't restrain myself from pulling until it led to the truth.

I rushed out of the café into the lobby before anyone could continue on to wherever they were headed and called out: "Hector. Hayley.

Aaron." All eyes focused on me. Those who didn't know me soon drifted back to their business while the three I'd addressed stood around me, with confusion, concern, surprise, and even anger in Aaron's case. I parted my lips to explain—but how could I articulate lines drawn instinctually to connect dots invisible to them? Instead, I persuaded them to sit down with me so I could explain how they were all connected.

Hector, the building's chief engineer, found us a conference room. There I learned Aaron worked on the seventh floor, Hayley regularly attended therapy for her substance-abuse recovery on the fourth floor, and Ramona worked on the ninth. They had passed each other in anonymous indifference, who knew how many times, unaware of the invisible ties among them. Hector spent time in every part of the building—but when he made an offhand comment about wasting half his time lately on the unoccupied thirteenth floor because the electric system there kept failing, a handful more puzzle pieces fell into place.

I explained how they'd all had related experiences that seemed disconnected and random until the moment I saw them together in the same place, until I reminded them of the electronic disturbances that had characterized their encounters, until they started to see the picture taking shape for themselves.

"You're all linked by this location," I said. "It sounds like we can trace everything you've gone through to something in this building."

"Hey, man, I don't know about that. It's pretty fucking weird, you know?" Hector said.

Hayley only shrugged, her eyes wide with recollections of terror.

"I don't know," Ramona said. "What if you're right? What do we do?"

Aaron scoffed. "There's nothing for us to do. I mean, let's just go to the damn thirteenth floor to look for your bug-eyed monsters. That's what you're after, right? That's the message you claim the universe is sending us? Something is broken on the thirteenth floor? Fine. Let's go fix it. When we don't find anything there other than empty office space, though, I'm going to have security drag you out of here, Keep. Then I'm calling the police for a restraining order against you. You're a lunatic."

"Aaron's right," Annetta said. "Not about the cops but checking the thirteenth floor. We've got no other leads, nowhere else to turn."

"No, we don't," I said.

Hector stood and pulled a ring of keys from his pocket. "All right, then, man, let's go."

Chapter Thirteen

Hector ushered us to the thirteenth floor a vast, gloomy expanse of cement floors, sparse fluorescent lights, and loose wiring protruding from walls and ceilings. Long rows of windows afforded views as far as Mount Misery and West Hills Preserve. I gravitated to the windows facing north and picked out the Preserve and the Northern State Parkway along its border, pulsing with cars like a clogged artery. Nothing at all stood between us and Long Island's highest elevation.

"I'm surprised they actually call this the thirteenth floor," I said. "Don't they know the superstition? You're supposed to skip thirteen to avoid bad luck."

"This floor has been nothing but bad luck. It's been unoccupied since we opened," Hector said. "We've had tenants lined up six times, but something always goes wrong last minute. Their funding falls through or they find better space and back out. Twice we failed the inspection due to electrical issues. They don't affect any other floor but this one. It's a fucking mystery. I've had my guys working on it for months, even called in outside electricians. No one can find anything wrong. Some days the power works. Other days, it doesn't. Some days we get a cell signal here. Other days, we don't. We use walkie-talkies, but even those crap out after a while. The company loses over a million a year on this vacancy."

"Maybe the men from Mars are stealing the electricity," Aaron said. "Except, oh, wait, I don't see anyone here, but us. You know what that means, don't you, Keep?" Aaron took out his cell phone, glanced at the screen. "It means I'm calling security. And look! I've got full bars."

Aaron tapped his phone screen. It flickered then brightened an intense white.

Ramona screamed.

Red light surged all around us, filling the space with the color of cartoon blood, blotting out the windows, erasing us from each other's view. An electric crackle and snap prefaced a yelp of pain from Aaron. Annetta clutched my hand and held tight to keep us from separating.

"What the hell?" Hector shouted. "Where's that damn light coming from?"

"I can't see anyone. Are you still here?" Hayley said, sounding on the verge of tears.

Ramona screamed again, a shriek of existential terror.

"No one move," I said. "We don't know what might be in here with us."

The brilliance of the red illumination faded. Shapes formed. We stood in the empty office space, everyone in the exact same place they'd occupied before the light. Hector clutched his cell phone, trying to make a call that wouldn't go through. Aaron had sagged to his knees, holding his bleeding right hand with his left. His cell phone lay smoking on the floor. Hayley cowered by a cement column. And Ramona… she stared into the open spaces and screamed again. I tried to see what she saw but couldn't. Not at first. But as the red light wavered and dimmed, a horrible scene coalesced in front of me.

"Do you see that?" I asked Annetta.

"Uh-huh," she said. "I wish I didn't."

"Who else sees it besides Ramona?" I shouted.

Hayley and Hector did. Aaron—I don't know what Aaron saw, if any of what transpired in that vacant space penetrated his awareness or if some embrace of oblivion protected him the way it had the night we found him in the woods. Aaron rose to his feet—then he levitated a few inches above the floor. He dangled like a puppet. A thin tendril attached to the back of his head snaked through the air, leading my eye to the Mothman, whose mouth hung agape, allowing his feathery proboscis to protrude. The creature looked haunted and ill, its double-lobed wings in tatters, its body withered to a chitinous, wicker mass. Its arms and legs stretched out to either side. Strands and clumps of webbing restrained it and locked it to the ceiling, a prisoner. Webs coated its eyes, except for one smoking hole where its light had burned through to reach us and show us all what was hidden right beside us. The webs draped and looped, coating the entire thirteenth floor, filling it with gauzy tubes and tunnels, coating the windows with a milky haze. Twelve-legged spiders scurried everywhere through and over the web structure, scuttling and hopping, too many for me to count. Behind the Mothman lurked a larger shape, a vast bulbous mass with the same awful twelve legs that shifted into view, revealing itself. A spider the size of an oil truck, its exoskeleton crusted with gnarled, horny growths like barnacles on an ancient whale. Three of its eight eyes were crusted and scabbed, blind. It moved without grace, lacking the arachnid efficiency of the younger and smaller creatures that raced around it. Its knobby joints creaked, and its mandibles clicked. Its rear segment and legs extended into a space visible through a gaping crack in the office wall, a crack not only material but sensory — ultrasensory — a fracture in reality.

"It is broken," Aaron said — not really Aaron, though, but the Mothman speaking through his voice, his body. "Small breakdowns become large breakdowns become catastrophes. What wills it so may come and go. None is broken or all is broken. I cannot see the flaws, the fractures, the splinters in the mind's eye."

"What the fuck is it doing to that guy?" Hector asked.

"He's borrowing him to tell us something," Annetta said.

"What? What does it want?" said Hayley, her voice high and quivering.

"It needs to see," I said. "Maybe then it can see the damage — the broken thing — and fix it. It needs to see clearly."

Ramona gave out a shriek and rushed at the Mothman, waving her hands, flailing at webs that snagged and clung to her body, gliding behind her like the ghost of a cape. She swatted away one of the mammoth spider's encrusted legs. Chunks of rime and exoskeleton spewed in a cloud from the impact. The small spiders frenzied around, coursing along web trails none of us could discern. The proboscis plunged into the back of Aaron's head throbbed.

"Clear me. Fix me. Fix the break. Change the tire. Repair the door. Replace the hinges. Unclog the gears. None is broken or all is broken," Aaron said in a monotone voice. His body hung in the air, feet dangling. One of his loafers dropped to the floor. His eyes rolled back in his head, and his mouth slacked open. "The splinters in the mind's eye must be removed. None is broken or all is broken."

Ramona grabbed a handful of webbing and ripped it away from the Mothman.

The giant spider jolted one of its three-pincered legs against her, knocking her on her back. The small ones swarmed her. She screamed, and her voice penetrated deeper than my ears, deeper than my brain, reaching my soul, and filling me with anguish. I rushed at the Mothman, ducking the flailing limbs of the ancient spider. I leapt a handful of small ones scuttling at my feet, stretched out my arms, heard Annetta shout my name, so muffled and far away, and then seized the thick webbing plastered over the Mothman's eyes. When I hit the floor and my knees buckled, I fell onto my side. The webbing cascaded onto me like wet comforters, blanketing me. It enveloped my face, filled my senses with unknown caustic aromas, coppery flavors. The webs glittered. The longer I stared at those shimmering flecks, the more they looked like stars, galaxies, entire universes enmeshed in the cloying, toxic material.

Then — red light consumed the world.

Everything vanished into a blinding field of sheer, seething red.

My sense of time broke. It seemed as if an eternity passed in the span of a single breath.

The red subsided. My sight cleared. The webs vanished. So did the multitude of twelve-legged spiders, along with the hoary ancient they served. The office space resumed its normal appearance. In the moment before the last, lingering horrors dissipated, I glimpsed the Mothman restored, freed from the web trap, wings spread to their full span, his twisty body rippling with renewed life, the crimson beams of his eyes fusing the split in reality through which the spiders had entered. As the last fraction of the crack vanished, thunder filled my ears.

The Mothman disappeared then too.

In a moment, Annetta reached my side and helped me to my feet.

Around us lay no hint of the madness we had encountered — except for the trauma it had left in its wake. Ramona curled up crying on the floor. Aaron face down and struggling to push himself onto his back. Tears streaming from Hayley's eyes. All color vanished from Hector's face, leaving him as pale as fresh paper, and he trembled.

"What… what the fuck was that?" he whispered.

I didn't answer. Neither did Annetta.

I needed to figure it out for myself before I could help anyone else understand.

"We have to get help," I said, then raising my voice, "Hector, call for help."

"Yeah, yeah," he said, eyeing his phone screen. "I've got bars."

He dialed one of the other engineers, told them to find the first aid kits, and haul ass to the thirteenth floor. When he ended the call, we waited.

Out the windows, I watched the very first rays of the setting sun paint the treetops around Mount Misery a bright, shimmering crimson.

Afterword

A nearly undetectable flaw in the iron link of a bridge support.

An invisible fracture in the substance of reality.

Life echoes itself, and sometimes, albeit rarely, those echoes add up to more than the source that generated them.

In my meetings with Ben, he posited a theory that the ancient, twelve-legged spider had mistakenly trapped the Mothman in its webs. Half-blind and nearing death, it stumbled across the crack between worlds, slipped through, and caught fresh prey, clouded by senility from realizing the damage it caused. The spiders weave. The Mothman preserves and protects, Ben suggested. He couldn't prove it. No one could. Were there many Mothmen showing up in different places or only one with the power to project its presence where it needed to appear? Had the Silver Bridge disaster been the result of a similar breach in reality, a crack left to burst like an unchecked tumor producing a minute but catastrophic break in our reality?

More and more questions no one can ever answer.

I vetted the material Ben and Annetta provided for this book with my own investigation, a follow-up that neither of them wished to undertake.

The Clementes refused to speak with me at first, but eventually Karina took one of my calls, hoping I could explain to her what had happened to Hector, who quit his job at the office tower and took on far less prestigious and lower paying work as a mechanic in his cousin's auto shop. She confirmed her account included in this book and acknowledged that the change in her husband related to it in some way, but he refused to speak of the matter.

Hayley Palmieri proved eager to talk and didn't seem to care if I believed her or not. She affirmed all that Ben and Annetta shared about the encounter on the thirteenth floor. She remains sober and in therapy, though she now sees a counselor in another building. She has spent time researching the realms of strange mysteries, coping with the trauma by demystifying it.

Aaron Reynolds refused to speak with me. When I explained the purpose of my call, he hung up on me then blocked my number. My calls to his friends who shared his experience went ignored. As far as I can ascertain, he continues to work in the office building and denies having ever had any encounter with the paranormal.

Ramona Cown proved unavailable. Her husband told me she checked herself into a six-month psychiatric treatment program and has, so far, refused to explain why even to him. He sounded despairing and heartbroken. Not knowing what, if anything, Ramona might've told him, I did not share any specifics with him.

The names, locations, and details have been altered for this book to deter anyone from intruding on the privacy of those involved or seeking the dangers described here. Except that is for Mount Misery, the West Hills Preserve, and Sweet Hollow Road. Those places exist as written here. They have a long history of weird events and legends, and, though I realize this story may amplify that reputation, I see no point in concealing them.

The thirteenth floor of the office tower remains vacant to this day, spurring legends of its own to further contribute to the mystery of the Mothman on Long Island.

Now and then, I see a spider. Whether or not one is always within three feet of me as Ben suggested, I cannot say. Only that when I see one I regard it closely and count the number of its legs. I am thankful that so far they have only twice numbered twelve.

James Chambers
Northport, NY

About the Author

James Chambers is a Bram Stoker Award® and Scribe Award-winning author and a four-time Bram Stoker Award nominee. He is the author of the short story collections *A Bright and Beautiful Eternal World*, described as "stellar" by *Publisher's Weekly*, *On the Night Border* and *On the Hierophant Road*, which received a starred review from *Booklist*, which called it "…satisfyingly unsettling"; the novella collection, *The Engines of Sacrifice*, and the novellas, *The Billabong Trail*, *The Devil in the Green*, *Kolchak and the Night Stalkers: The Faceless God*, *Three Chords of Chaos*, and many others, as well as the original graphic novel, *Kolchak the Night Stalker: The Forgotten Lore of Edgar Allan Poe*. His short stories have appeared in anthologies and publications in multiple genres, including crime, fantasy, horror, pulp, science fiction, steampunk, and more. He edited the Bram Stoker Award-nominated anthologies, *Under Twin Suns: Alternate Histories of the Yellow Sign* and *A New York State of Fright* as well as *Even in the Grave*, an anthology of ghost stories, and *Where the Silent Ones Watch*.

His website is: www.jameschambersonline.com.

About the Artist

Until his decades-long disappearance, JW Harp was known for his trippy underground comic strip *Captain Thetan*, about a seafarer who controls reality for himself and others. This otherworldly character appeared in a dozen issues of the classic rare underground zine *Sandanista Romp*. JW has reemerged thanks largely to eSpec Books' Systema Paradoxa series. In 2023, JW started Skilletfire Studios with comic-book author Scott Eckelaert. Under the Skilletfire Studios mantle, JW has produced the graphic novel *Boylon Heights*, and the *Gimme Five Comics* series. Since its launch, *Gimme Five Comics* has included work by Artyom Topilin, Elena Cerisciola, John L. French, Keith Lansdale, and Joe R. Lansdale with more to come.

JW grew up in the seedy parts of South Carolina, which is all of it. He feels part Canadian and part Costa Rican these days. He lives in North Carolina. Please get in touch with him at jwharp@skilletfire.com.

artist's rendition of Mothman

MOTHMAN

ORIGINS: First sighted in Point Pleasant, West Virginia. There are various theories of its origin, such as an undiscovered species, an extraterrestrial being, a supernatural creature, or harbinger of catastrophe. Other sightings have been reported world-wide, including Chicago and as far away as Moscow.

DESCRIPTION: Despite the name, this humanoid creature is described with more avian features, believed to more closely resemble an owl than a moth. It is said to be slender and male, standing between six and seven feet tall. The wings are reported as white or brown with a span of ten to fifteen feet. Those who have experienced first-hand encounters have no details of the creature's features other than the eyes, which are large and red, glowing like a reflector. The eyes are also reported to be hypnotic. Its body coloration is described as white or brown or black, but mostly dark. While not very agile on the ground, moving with an awkward walking gait, Mothman is said to be able to take flight like a helicopter and fly at a rate of a hundred miles an hour.

LIFE CYCLE: Unknown.

HISTORY: In November of 1966, reports started to come in of a flying humanoid creature seen in the region of Point Pleasant, West Virginia. The first account was by the owner of a missing German Shepherd that disappeared after chasing after two glowing red eyes in the forest. After that, on the night of the 15th two young couples were out driving on route 62 near the abandoned WWII munitions plant the locals dubbed "the TNT area," when they saw this giant winged humanoid. They sped away only to be chased by the creature, which shrieked after them.

When the local paper picked up the story over a hundred similar encounters were reported over the ensuing thirteen months. There were claims that witnesses were visited by "Men in Black" and dissuaded from sharing their experiences. The accounts died down following the collapse of the Silver Bridge, a tragedy where forty-six people lost their lives.

Popular opinion was that the creature appeared as a harbinger of the event, trying to warn the townfolk, a theory that took on global significance when those in Russia reported their own sighting in Moscow right before the 1999 apartment bombings and preceding the Chernobyl reactor meltdown. Miners in Germany claimed Mothman chased them away from their shaft right before it collapsed, and two photographs circulated placing Mothman in New York during the 9/11 disaster.

Reports continued to come in over the ensuing years, though not in the volume prior to December 1967, including a photograph claimed to be the Mothman taking flight circulated in 2016, and a rash of reported sightings in Chicago in 2017.

In 2002, Point Pleasant organized the first annual Mothman Festival, which continues to this day, flooding the town with three times its normal population for one weekend in September. In 2003 the town erected a Mothman statue by artist Bob Roach, and in 2005 the Mothman Museum and Research Center opened its doors.

THEORIES: Aside from the belief that Mothman could be an extra-terrestrial or a supernatural being, those more skeptical theorize that the sightings were no more than various avians mistaken for something "other," primarily either the sandhill crane, a great blue heron, or a snowy owl, all of which are large birds with wide wingspans. And the photographs claimed to be Mothman have been dismissed as Photoshopped fakes, a bird taking flight with a kill, or a bit of loose metal hanging off a bridge. But the legend and the sightings persist.

CAPTURE THE CRYPTIDS!

Cryptid Crate is a monthly subscription box filled with various cryptozoology and paranormal themed items to wear, display and collect. Expect a carefully curated box filled with creeptastic pieces from indie makers and artisans pertaining to bigfoot, sasquatch, UFOs, ghosts, and other cryptid and mysterious creatures (apparel, decor, media, etc).

http://CryptidCrate.com

www.ingramcontent.com/pod-product-compliance
Lightning Source LLC
Chambersburg PA
CBHW031415310726
48971CB00003B/871